THE KING'S NAMESAKE
A TALE OF CARISBROOK CASTLE

KING CHARLES I ON THE EVE OF THE BATTLE OF EDGHILL.

AFTER CHARLES LANDSEER.

The King's Namesake.

THE KING'S NAMESAKE
A TALE OF CARISBROOK CASTLE

BY

CATHERINE MARY PHILLIMORE

" All heads must come
To the cold tomb ;
Only the actions of the just
Smell sweet and blossom in the dust."
ROBERT SHIRLEY.

WILDSIDE PRESS

Originally published 1873
Reissue 1928

PRINTED IN GREAT BRITAIN

LIST OF ILLUSTRATIONS

PREFACE

THE history of the Great Rebellion furnishes many interesting incidents on which to found a tale; but there is hardly any part of it so surrounded with romance as that period during which King Charles the First was a captive in Carisbrook Castle.

There is much of deep pathos associated with this epoch in the life of the unhappy monarch, and, a few years ago, a book was published, purporting to be a true historical account of his imprisonment in the Isle of Wight, and containing fifteen genuine letters from the King himself to Captain Titus,* at that time one of his most loyal and faithful servants. This publication is entitled,

A Narrative of the Attempted Escape of Charles the First from Carisbrook Castle :

By George Hillier ;

and the Royal letters given in it were deciphered and published, for the first time, in 1852.

For many of the incidents, which are historical, related in the following tale, the writer is indebted to this book, as for a great many useful details respecting the King's pursuits during his captivity, and the means employed by his loyal friends for his release.

Much information has also been gleaned from that

---

* Captain Titus was the author of the celebrated pamphlet, *Killing no Murder*, published in 1657, by which he endeavoured to prove that killing the Protector would be both a lawful and meritorious act.

curious and valuable contemporaneous document, *John Ashburnham's Narrative.*

The opinion of the world is so apt to be swayed by what is termed the success of a man's life, that justice has, perhaps, scarcely been done to the patient heroism displayed by King Charles throughout his adverse fortunes.

If this short story should be the means of throwing further light upon those essentially Christian virtues which adorned his character, the pains which have been spent upon it will be more than repaid.

THE KING'S NAMESAKE
A TALE OF CARISBROOK CASTLE

CHAPTER I

" He has doff'd the silk doublet the breastplate to bear,
He has placed the steel cap o'er his long flowing hair,
From his belt to his stirrup his broadsword hangs down,—
Heaven shield the brave gallant that fights for the Crown !

" For the rights of fair England that broadsword he draws,
Her King is his leader, her Church is his cause ;
His watchword is honour, his pay is renown,—
God strike with the gallant that strikes for the Crown ! "

Rokeby, Canto. V. s. xx.

THE autumn of 1647 was fast drawing to a close, yet still
the eye lingered with delight over the many-hued foliage
which brightened the landscape with rich tints of red and
gold.

It was one of those quiet October days, which seemed
to invite calm reflection and sober thoughts, when the
mind is first captivated by the aspect of nature, glorious
even in its decay, and then led on to muse upon the short-
lived beauty of all earthly things.

Such thoughts were passing through the mind of a tall,
delicate-looking lady, as she walked slowly towards her
home, a small house on the outskirts of the little village of
Carisbrook. She was clad in deep mourning, and her
history was a sad, though unhappily not an uncommon,
one in those troubled times. Her husband had been killed

9

fighting for the King at the battle of Naseby, and now she
was comparatively destitute, with a family of three
children to educate and support.

The daughter of a clergyman, she had married at twenty-
one a country gentleman, who possessed a small property
in the Isle of Wight. The marriage had been one of the
purest affection, and for many years they had lived a life
of unchequered happiness. Three children were born to
them : two sons and a daughter. They were not rich, but
they had an income sufficient for their wants ; and her
husband, who had no particular profession, employed his
time and added to his small means by farming. He took
no interest in politics, did not follow the discontented
murmurings and dissensions of the Parliament, and was
quite unaware of the increasing unpopularity of the King.
He was therefore taken by surprise when the King's
standard was set up at Nottingham, and all loyal subjects
were invited to gather round it and defend the King from
his enemies.

Arthur Harcourt was a Royalist in the truest accepta-
tion of the word ; he would never have dreamed of ques-
tioning his sovereign's command. " Fear God, honour
the King," was his family motto ; and he would almost
as soon have thought of proving false to the first injunction
as to the last. Collecting what few followers he had, and
bidding a hasty adieu to his wife and children, he set off
without delay to join the Royal army at Nottingham.

" We shall soon put the rebels to the rout," he said to
his wife ; " so keep up a good heart : pray for me, my
darling, and let the children pray too, and for our King.
If all goes well, please God, I shall soon return ; if not, I
am in His hands. Teach the children our motto,—no
Harcourt ever proved false to it yet ! God bless you, my
darling, and farewell."

For three years he fought gallantly for the King, and

then came the "fatal field of Naseby," where the Royalists
were cut to pieces ; and one only of Arthur Harcourt's
small company of faithful followers returned from the
battle, wounded, travel-stained, and almost famished,
with the terrible news that his brave master had been
killed in the act of covering the King's retreat. The
distress and anguish of his poor wife can easily be
imagined ; she loved her husband with the clinging, fond
love of her gentle nature, and had never vexed him once
during the happy years they had lived together. Now he
was gone she would have to struggle with life alone, in
these perilous times, and she must see that her children
were worthy of the name they bore. However, beneath
that gentle, winning exterior, Alice Harcourt had a brave
spirit. She was a woman of high principles, early instilled
into her by a pious father, and had always held fast by
them. Hitherto she had been assailed by comparatively
few trials ; now that they seemed to be coming upon her,
she resolved to hold firm, by the grace of God, to these
good principles. Her children, Charles, Arthur, and
Frances, at the time of their father's departure for the war,
were too young to be of much assistance to her in her
anxiety and trouble ; but now she was beginning to reap
the fruits of the careful training which she had given
them, and she found in them a daily solace and a daily
interest.

Charles, the eldest, so called because he was born on the
King's birthday, was tall and slight, with blue eyes and
fair hair like his mother. At the time of his father's death
he was in his fifteenth year, and perhaps the shock which
it gave him, and the additional weight of responsibility
which was thus thrown upon him, rendered him more than
usually grave and thoughtful. He had never delighted
in the perilous adventures which were the favourite
pursuit of his brother Arthur ; but on occasions of real

danger, in addition to great courage and determination, he displayed a coolness and firmness which rendered his assistance invaluable.

Arthur, who was only one year younger than his brother, was eager and impetuous, caring chiefly for, and excelling in, all out-door pursuits. His great delight was in sailing : often and often would he persuade some old fisherman to take him out in his boat, spend all the day fishing, and return home triumphant with some trophies of his sport, which his good-natured old companion would allow him to take to his mother.

Frances, the youngest of the three children, was the image of her mother, and her beauty was of that true Saxon type which we never weary of, however often we may see it. She was very fair, with long golden hair, which she wore in plaits round her head ; and her mother was so proud of it, that she would not allow it to be hidden away under the little prim cap, then generally worn. Her eyebrows were very finely pencilled, and her eyes, grey rather than blue, had that pensive look which is the peculiar charm of grey eyes ; her nose was straight, more of the Grecian that the Roman type, and there was a great deal of expression in her mouth ; her smile was rare, but very sweet ; her skin was exceedingly fair, and her colouring delicate pink and white, like the inside of a shell. She was tall for her age, and inherited her mother's dignity of carriage. With regard to her character, although sweet-tempered and docile, she had her father's fearless spirit, and her courage rose in the presence of any danger ; her feelings were quick, her heart warm and affectionate. Although not old enough at the time of her father's death to appreciate fully the extent of her loss, she was quite sensible of the blank it made in her home, and shed many bitter tears in secret when she thought she should no more feel his kind hand stroking her head, or hear him, in the full tones of his rich, deep voice, bid her be a good girl, and cheer up her mother while he was away.

All the children were devotedly attached to the home in which they had been born and brought up; and as travelling for pleasure was a rare event in those times, they had not seen much beyond it. Now and then they had been taken to the annual fair at Newport, or to Carisbrook to see their maternal grandfather, who was vicar of that parish. These visits were a great comfort to Madam Harcourt, for Dr. Russell was the best possible type of the clergy of those days. Pious and benevolent, he had the gentle gravity of manner and demeanour which indicates a mind chiefly occupied with grave and solemn subjects, while he bore in his face the outward token of the inward peace resulting from a long life of holiness. Moreover, he had the reputation of being a very learned divine, and resisted steadily the mistaken opinion, that careful study and deep research were carnal weapons unmeet for spiritual warfare.

Madam Harcourt's father had given her a careful and religious education, and had ever been her wisest and kindest counsellor, to whom she had resorted in all her difficulties during her husband's absence. Now that the terrible news of his death had reached her, she resolved to fly to her father for advice and consolation in this her hour of trial. There was the additional reason for deciding upon this course, that she could no longer afford to live in her present home. The expenses consequent upon the war had fallen heavily upon her husband. Like every good Royalist of those days, he had lent large sums of money to the King; he had even melted down his plate, as his Royal master's necessity became more urgent; all that remained to Madam Harcourt and her children was a small pittance of seventy pounds a year. She determined, therefore, with many pangs, to sell the home where she had lived so happily for many years, and to take a small house in Carisbrook, where she might be near her father and benefit by his protection.

The resolve once taken, she acted upon it without delay. The chief difficulty consisted in finding a purchaser for her present residence. However, Mr. Newland, of Newport, who had been her husband's great friend, came to her assistance and purchased her small property at a little above its real value, for his old friend's sake. With this addition to her income, Madam Harcourt was able to provide herself with a small house in Carisbrook village, where she could, as she thought, live the rest of her life in quietness, striving to teach her children to be loyal servants of their King, cherishing the memory of him whom she had lost, and praying for the cause he had died for. At all events, her state of widowhood and poverty would for the future exempt her from taking any active part in the Civil War. One of the many advantages of her scheme consisted in the fact of there being an excellent grammar-school at Newport, within a mile of Carisbrook, where her sons might be educated at a moderate cost by two Royalist gentlemen, a certain Mr. William Hopkins and his son.

At length her plans were all finally arranged, the day of departure arrived, and, accompanied by her children, a faithful man-servant, the one who had returned from Naseby, and a maid-servant, who had been in her service since her marriage she bade adieu to her much-loved home.

Thus towards the end of the year 1645 she began her new life in a small house on the outskirts of Carisbrook village, and bravely prepared herself to face at once her altered circumstances. Her two boys were entered as day scholars at the grammar-school at Newport, which was within an easy distance of Carisbrook, and during their absence

Frances was her chief delight and solace. She taught her what little she herself knew,—for in those days women were not very learned, and read but few books save the Bible, in which they were carefully instructed ; and the rest of her time was devoted to household avocations, varied with working tapestry or spinning, and ministering to the wants of the poor in her father's parish.

The vast and ruinous changes which were at that period taking place in the ecclesiastical affairs of the kingdom had not yet found their way to the Isle of Wight, nor had Madam Harcourt's father shared as yet the fate of most of his brother clergy, who had been ejected from their benefices.

The beautiful liturgy of our Church was still retained in the old parish church of Carisbrook, which remained untouched by the hands of either Presbyterian or Independent. These, while they agitated the whole of England with their disputes over the spoils of the Church, agreed only in the destruction of everything which had served to adorn her material fabrics. But this exemption from the general calamities was not destined to last much longer. In the following year the Parliament established, by an ordinance, the Presbyterian government of the Church. This was a death-blow to the few Prelatical clergy, as they were called, who had hitherto been left unmolested. Worse was in store for them. Hardly had the Presbyterian Directory been formally established in place of the Liturgy than the Independents came into power, and then the confusion was inextricable and the misery universal : clergy were driven from their homes ; the use of the Prayer-book was interdicted, under heavy penalties, in private houses ; churches were dismantled, often even destroyed, and sepulchres defaced. These were the men who complained of the intolerance of Archbishop Laud.

They were indeed

> " Such as do build their faith upon
> The holy text of pike and gun ;
> Decide all controversies by
> Infallible artillery ;
> And prove their doctrine orthodox
> By apostolic blows and knocks ;
> Call fire, and sword, and desolation,
> A godly thorough Reformation,
> Which always must be carried on,
> And still be doing, never done :
> As if Religion were intended
> For nothing else but to be mended." *

Dr. Russell could not hope to escape the storm which overwhelmed his brethren. He was also driven from his benefice, and the church which he loved and in which he had ministered so many years shared the unhappy fate of all the churches in the land.

He would not, however, leave Carisbrook, on account of his daughter and her children. Had it been possible, Madam Harcourt would only too gladly have asked him to share her home ; but it was so small that it would barely accommodate herself and her family, so Dr. Russell took a small lodging close at hand, and spent much of the day in the society of his daughter and grandchildren.

When the first fury of his assailants had somewhat subsided, he was able occasionally to minister in secret to the spiritual wants of many of his former parishioners.

The affairs of the King were in as disastrous a condition as the affairs of the Church. He had been compelled to fly from Oxford to the Scottish army at Newark, and in the summer of 1647 the hopes of the Royalist party were crushed by a terrible blow. It became known that, through the treachery of the Scots, the King had actually fallen into the hands of his enemies, having been seized at Holmby Castle on the 3rd of June. The fear, however,

* *Hudibras*, Part I, Canto 3.

of any immediate personal violence to the King was soon set at rest, for it was evident that, in the daily-increasing national confusion, a large body of men had begun to desire fervently the re-establishment of the ancient form of government under which their ancestors had enjoyed happiness and tranquillity.   The King was, therefore, brought south by the army, in order that he might come to terms with the Parliament, and finally lodged, with an appearance of dignity and freedom, at Hampton Court. But this lull in the state of affairs was of very short duration.   Rumours reached the King that Cromwell had a secret intention of assassinating him, so on the 11th of November in that same year his escape was contrived by three of his most loyal and attached servants, whose names are well known in history, and he fled to Titchfield, the residence of Lady Southampton.

This is the period at which our story begins ; and it was on the 12th of this month, as Madam Harcourt was on her way home from the village, that her two boys, who had just come back from Newport, rushed up to her with eager looks.

" Mother," shouted Arthur, " we have seen two Cavaliers, two real Cavaliers ; I'm sure of it, for, in spite of their disguise, they had none of the sneaking look of Cromwell's Puritans about them ; and we saw their long hair escaping from under their hideous steeple-crowned hats.   They were exactly like the picture of our father that you have, mother ; and I heard one say to the other, ' Now he is safe out of their clutches, we must take care he does not fall into them again ' "

Madam Harcourt started.

" Who could they mean ? " she said, turning to Charles.

A grave expression came over his thoughtful face as he answered—

" I cannot say.   They seemed to me to have some

B

weighty business on hand, for they were so earnestly
engaged in conversation, as their horses walked slowly
along the road, that they did not see us till they were
quite close, and then one of them called to me and asked
me how far it was to Newport, and where he could find
the Governor of the island ; he had heard he was in
Newport. Just as I was about to answer, I saw a man on
horseback coming from the opposite direction, and in
another minute I recognised Colonel Hammond. ' Sir,' I
said, pointing him out, ' the Governor is at this moment
advancing towards you.' Whereupon they exchanged
looks, and seemed very much confused. Then presently,
after whispering together a few minutes, they saluted
Colonel Hammond, who had now ridden up to them, and
said they had something very important to say to him ;
whereupon they all three rode away together. We
watched them awhile, and they had hardly gone a few
paces when we observed the Governor suddenly rein up
his horse and look frightened at something they said, and
then they set off at a round trot towards the castle."

Madam Harcourt was much puzzled by this story. She
was at a loss to conceive what these two Cavaliers, if
Cavaliers they were, could have to communicate to Colonel
Hammond, who had been appointed Governor only a
few weeks ago by the Parliament, and the scrap of conversation which Arthur reported filled her with a vague,
undefined feeling of alarm. Colonel Hammond was not a
stranger to her, she had known him all her life. He was
the nephew of her father's most intimate friend Dr.
Hammond, one of the King's chaplains, and from childhood upwards there had been constant intercourse between
the two families, which on the side of Colonel Hammond
had developed itself into a strong attachment, which Alice
Russell was unable to return. An estrangement followed,
then came her marriage with Arthur Harcourt, and she

had not seen Colonel Hammond since, but she had heard that, mortified and disappointed, he had embraced the side of the Parliament in all political discussions, and when the war broke out had fought in their army against the King. Finally, in order to link himself to their cause still more closely, he had married the daughter of the famous Hampden. She had died some years previously, but in consequence of this close connection with their party, he was promoted by Cromwell to the then important post of Governor of the Isle of Wight. When Madam Harcourt heard of his appointment she was much troubled, fearing lest he should attempt to renew their former intimacy, for if she disliked him before, her dislike was now increased tenfold by his conduct during the war. An instant's reflection, however, assured her that he would have no wish to risk his character in the eyes of the Parliament by an alliance with the widow of a known Cavalier. She hoped, however, never to see him, for the very sight of him was hateful to her.

She felt very anxious to communicate to her father the tidings the children had brought, and, bidding them follow her and not reveal to any one what they had overheard, she began to walk quickly towards Dr. Russell's lodging. She was within a few yards of the door when, looking up, she beheld, to her astonishment and dismay, Colonel Hammond actually standing on the doorstep waiting to enter. His countenance was much troubled, his dress disordered, his boots bespattered with mud, and he clutched a paper tightly in his hand. She stood petrified ; he saw her, his face brightened for an instant, then its expression as suddenly changed, and he bowed stiffly to her. The next moment the door opened and he entered.

Madam Harcourt returned to her home deeply perplexed to see him at her father's door in such evident discomposure, and she dreaded lest there should be some ground for the fears which her children's story had excited in her mind.

Her house looked upon the keep of Carisbrook Castle, which frowned upon the village from an elevation of some sixty feet. This fortress had not yet played its destined part in the melancholy annals of those times, but was even then a building of remarkable history Originally the private dwelling of some wealthy Roman, it had been converted into a Norman stronghold by William Fitz-Osborne, Earl of Hereford, first Lord of the Island after the Conquest. The gateway, flanked by two large towers, still bore the arms of Woodville, whose relationship to the wife of Edward IV procured him the office of Governor ; while its outer gate presented the sculptured initials of Queen Elizabeth, who added the last fortifications.

Weak are the devices of men ! Little did the great Queen foresee that the fortress which she had made so strong against the foreign foe would be used, before the lapse of half a century, as a prison in which her second successor to the throne would be confined by his rebellious subjects.

In the little garden over which this massive building towered, Madam Harcourt met Frances, who ran up to her eagerly.

" O mother ! " she said, " what do you think ? A little while ago three gentlemen on horseback dashed up the hill to the castle as hard as they could go, and in about half an hour's time one came down quite alone, and went into the village. I asked Nicholas who he was, and he said it was Colonel Hammond, the new Governor, a horrid Puritan."

" O hush, Frances ! " said Madam Harcourt ; " such rash words may bring great trouble upon us, and upon the cause we hold so dear. My mind misgives me sorely as to the errand of these gentlemen to the Governor."

She entered, and the children followed, quiet and subdued. The short November day was nearly over, and Madam Harcourt ordered supper to be prepared, as her boys were hungry from their walk ; the evening slipped peacefully away, and, soothed by her wonted occupation, she almost forgot the agitating occurrence of the afternoon.

It was a perfectly calm, frosty night, and the silence was only occasionally disturbed by the distant baying of a watch-dog, or by a faint echo of the hum of life in the village. Presently Madam Harcourt heard the even tread of a footstep on the walk outside, which, as it drew nearer, she recognised as her father's. In a few minutes he knocked at the door.

" Charles, it is your grandfather ; run and let him in," said Madam Harcourt.

Dr. Russell in another moment was in the room. There was a cloud on his placid face, and signs of great agitation which were unusual in a man of his calm and even temperament.

" Alice," he said, " I have important news to tell you."

" Good, I trust," said Alice, striving to quiet the fears which would arise in spite of all her efforts.

" God grant it may be good ! " replied her father. " His Majesty has escaped from Hampton Court."

There was for an instant a dead silence, which Arthur was the first to break by saying——

" Hurrah ! God save the King ! That was what those gentlemen were talking about. Where is he, grandfather ? have his own party rallied ? has Prince Rupert joined him ? "

A look from his mother stopped this torrent of questions ; and, still with the same vague fear at her heart, she said—

" Father, which direction did his Majesty take on leaving Hampton Court ? "

" He is now in these parts," said Dr. Russell ; " not very far off, I imagine, but I know not the exact place

of his concealment. I would, however, he were going to
remain where he is at present, till he can make his escape
out of this turbulent kingdom, for I fear he is going to
trust himself in very unsafe hands."

"He is not coming here!" said Madam Harcourt,
feeling that all her forebodings were about to be realised.

"I fear so; and I will give you my reason," said her
father. "While I was sitting in my room this afternoon,
I heard a loud knock at the door, and presently I was told
that a gentleman wanted to speak with me. I asked who
it was, but before any answer could be made he pushed
past the woman who had opened the door, and strode into
my room. Alice, it was Robert Hammond! I should
have felt greater displeasure at his having thus forced
himself upon me had I not been struck by the look of
mingled terror and perplexity which was upon his face.
Time has made many changes in him since I last saw him;
he has lost that open, ingenuous expression which he had
as a boy, and it has been succeeded by a look of restless
dissatisfaction and uneasiness. However, I had but little
time to observe him, for he began at once: 'Dr. Russell,
you were once a kind friend to me, you are still the dear
friend of my uncle, and I entreat you by that friendship
to give me your advice and assistance in a most important
matter. Do not look so coldly upon me because I have
been compelled by conscientious scruples to take a different
view to yours of the present distracted state of affairs;
perhaps, too, I may be able to assist you where your
dearest interests are concerned.' 'If you need advice,'
I said, 'tell me what your trouble is, and I will do my
best to help you, but I have no wish to enter into political
discussions.' He paused a moment, and then, changing
entirely his incoherent manner, he went on. 'You know
I have been lately appointed Governor of this island, and
this morning I rode into Newport to meet some gentle-

men and officers, on business connected with my new
office. On my return I was met in the road and accosted
by two gentlemen, who said they had urgent business
with me. They were Cavaliers, the personal attendants
of King Charles, I afterwards discovered ; they informed
me that he had escaped last night from Hampton Court,
fearing assassination, that he was now in a place of concealment not far off, waiting to know if I, as a loyal
subject, would afford him protection and a place of
safety from his enemies in the Isle of Wight. They
accompanied me back to the castle, and are waiting to
know what answer they shall take back from me to the
King. What shall I do ? Surely never was such a
responsibility thrust upon any man.' (You may imagine,
Alice, with what eagerness I listened to this tale ; but
my heart misgave me when I perceived his lukewarmness
and selfish fears. I saw, however, that since so fearful a
risk had been already run, and everything was at stake, I
must make a vigorous endeavour to bring him to view the
matter in its proper light.) ' I fear me,' I said, ' you are
not the Robert Hammond that I recollect, who, in the
enthusiasm of his boyhood, would gladly have risked the
last drop of his blood for his Royal master, or I would
descant upon the high privilege which is now granted you
of succouring him in his distress. Still, changed as you
are, I will not believe you so lost as not to perceive the
sacred duties ; honour and hospitality involved in this
case. As a soldier, a gentleman, and a Christian, surely
there can be no doubt that either you must promise to
entertain his Majesty in all good faith and freedom, so
long as it shall please him to stay here, or else not to reveal
a word of what has been told you until he is in a place of
security elsewhere. I do not dwell upon the great benefit
which you might confer upon the country in the settlement of the divisions and distractions which abound in

every corner, by enabling the King to act and treat with the Parliament unfettered by the restraint of a prison.' He seemed much moved, and was silent for a few minutes. At last he said, ' But what message shall I send ? I am distracted with doubt.' Then I saw it would be best and safest to keep his Majesty out of his hands, so I urged him to send back a message to the following effect : ' That if it pleased the King to put himself into his hands, whatever he could expect from a person of honour or honesty his Majesty should have it made good by him.'*

" This appeared to me the only way out of the difficulty, so much being already involved ; for while, on the one hand, Hammond's honour was thereby engaged to preserve the King's person in safety, and at liberty, supposing his Majesty were to come to the island ; on the other hand, the cold and guarded nature of the message would probably suggest doubts to the King as to whether Hammond were fit to be trusted with so grave a responsibility.

" He seemed well satisfied with it himself, it set his scruples at rest and delivered him for the present out of his difficulty ; so he thanked me warmly, and left me apparently much easier in mind."

Dr. Russell ceased speaking, and Madam Harcourt heaved a deep sigh.

" I hope all will be well," she said ; " I mistrust Colonel Hammond, for, although meaning well, he is weak and unstable as water, and not to be depended on whenever his own interest is at stake."

Just then the stillness outside was broken by the clatter of horses' hoofs, as if some one were riding down from the castle at a rapid rate.

" It must be the messengers returning to the King," said Dr. Russell, as he walked quickly to the window. With the help of the bright moonlight he was able to

* See Ashburnham's *Narrative and Vindication*, Vol. II, p. 115.

discern plainly three figures on horseback advancing at a brisk trot.

" There are three men," said Dr. Russell in a tone of alarm. " I trust Robert Hammond has not proved a traitor, and insisted upon accompanying them back to the King's hiding-place."

An expression implying " God forbid ! " came over Madam Harcourt's face, but she said nothing, and the interest at stake was far too grave to admit of any conjecture upon this point, so with a heavy heart Dr. Russell bade his daughter good night, and returned to his home.

On the following morning rumours were current in the village of King Charles's escape from London, and his supposed intention of taking up his abode in Carisbrook Castle, in state, and at liberty ; that the rebellion would at last come to an end, and the Parliament be brought to terms.

The islanders rejoiced, for they were faithful to their sovereign in spite of his misfortunes.

Madam Harcourt's servant Nicholas, who had fought at Naseby, was wild with excitement when these rumours reached his ear, and he rushed out into the village to pick up what news he could. All his Cavalier instincts revived ; he longed to be on the scene of action, and to be the first to shout, " Long live the King ! " when his Majesty entered Newport. But he was not likely to gain much satisfactory information in this chance manner, so after one or two unsuccessful efforts he made his way to Dr. Russell's lodging, to find out from the cook, who was a friend of his, if any tidings had reached her master. And now there seemed more chance of his curiosity being gratified, for the cook readily informed him that Colonel Hammond had despatched a special messenger to Dr. Russell ; moreover, she continued, her master had left Carisbrook early that morning, entrusting her with a letter for Madam Harcourt, which she gave to Nicholas.

It was carefully folded and sealed, and Nicholas hastened home with it, burning to know its contents. He delivered it at once to Madam Harcourt who was breakfasting with her children, and made many efforts to remain in the room till it was opened; but this Madam Harcourt thought it not prudent to permit, and having dismissed him, she opened the letter, and read it over first to herself. It was as follows, in the formal style of those times :

" For the honoured hands of my dear daughter Alice Harcourt, these.

" A special messenger has just arrived from the Governor to acquaint me that his Majesty King Charles passed the night at Cowes, and will in the course of this morning ride through Newport on his way to Carisbrook, where he is to reside, as prisoner or king, I know not. In these present circumstances I think it best to go in search of his Majesty's chaplain, Dr. Hammond, and thereby a double end will be gained, for he will keep watch upon his nephew, and at the same time his presence will greatly minister to the King's comfort. I fear me Robert Hammond has acted a dishonourable part, for he insisted upon accompanying the King's gentlemen back to Titchfield, where the King was in hiding, and forced himself upon the King, who had thus no other alternative except that of placing himself in the Governor's hand. God grant Colonel Hammond may have no treacherous designs upon his Majesty's liberty ! "

Madam Harcourt's contenance fell as she read this letter, and her son Charles, rising hastily, asked if it contained any bad news. For all response she put the letter into his hands, which he read eagerly.

" O mother, never fear," he cried ; " if the King has enemies, he has also many faithful and loyal supporters, the sons of those who have shed their blood in his cause. Perhaps great good may come of his sojourn here, and that cantankerous Parliament be brought to terms at last. At all events, if things turn out untowardly we can easily contrive his escape here on the sea-coast ; he shall not fall again into the hands of his enemies, and God will defend the right."

Madam Harcourt looked up at her son with a ray of hope in her face.

" There is a great deal in what you say," she answered ; " we may yet be of use to the King. I thought," she added, with a gentle sigh, " all that was over for me, but what there is left that I can give him is gladly at his service."

" Mother," cried Arthur and Frances both in a breath, " we may go to Newport to see the King come, may we not ? "

" Yes," said Madam Harcourt, " if you and Charles will take great care of Frances, supposing there should be a crowd. I shall stay here, where I can also see his Majesty ride up to the castle ; there is some pleasure in the thought that we shall be so near him. But you had better lose no time ; he will be early at Newport, as Cowes can afford no proper resting-place for him."

In a very short time the children were ready, and set off walking, or rather running the greater part of the way, to Newport. They directed their steps towards the market-place, through which the King must inevitably pass on his way to Carisbrook. Here they found a good many people collected, some discoursing apart, but most of them having taken up their position on either side of the street. There seemed to be a sort of vague feeling of alarm at what might be the possible issue of King Charles's escape to their island ; by this time all the Newport townspeople were acquainted with the fact, but for the most part joy at seeing him, mingled with curiosity, were the pre-dominant feelings.

It was a lovely day, bright and mild, and in spite of

the advanced season of the year there were still some roses and myrtles to be seen in the gardens in front of the small houses in the country town of Newport. Before leaving home that morning Frances had taken good care to select from the few remaining flowers in their garden a beautiful damask rose. Her brothers thought she intended to wear it, and were rather surprised to see her carry it in her hand, carefully shielding it lest it should be hit or brushed by the crowd. However, they asked her no questions, and presently the three children took their places also close to the edge of the pavement.

The eager expectations of the people were not destined to be damped by delay, for in a very short time the sound of horses' hoofs announced the approach of the King and his party. He arrived at a brisk trot, but, with that unfailing courtesy which never deserted him, even in the darkest hour of adversity, on perceiving the crowd of people, and guessing their object, he at once drew bridle and made his horse walk slowly through the market-place.

Whatever diversity of opinion respecting him there may have been amongst the townspeople, all were favourably impressed by this mark of courtesy, and this impression developed itself into a deeper feeling of awe and respect when they beheld his erect and noble mien and the stately grace with which he acknowledged their salutations, for they had not yet been taught by the Puritans that any respect paid to their sovereign was a crime.

The good feelings towards King Charles were destined to become enthusiastic before the scene of the morning was over. A young and lovely girl advanced out of the crowd, and, curtseying to the ground, presented him with a beautiful damask rose.

" Sire," she said, " may God bless you and deliver you out of all your troubles, and may He bring the counsel of the wicked to nought, for our dear Lord's sake ! "

The King was deeply moved by this sudden and unexpected occurrence, and, taking the rose with one hand while he uncovered his head with the other—

" We thank you heartily," he said, " for this testimony of your good-will towards us, and, if it should please God to grant your petition, we will not forget this your kindness towards us in the hour of our adversity."

The people gazed with deep interest upon the scene before them. The King uncovered, with all his long curling hair mingling with his horse's mane, as he stooped to address the beautiful girl kneeling at his stirrup ; the refined majesty of his face, which had once worn a look of pride almost amounting to disdain, was now, since his troubles had come upon him, softened by an expression of patient dignity and resignation. There was also a moisture in his eye as he beheld the lovely girl who, overwrought by excitement and the unlooked-for delight of being thus addressed, could not restrain her tears of joy. The people raised a shout of " Long live King Charles ! we will save him from his enemies ! " and, the enthusiasm increasing, hats were thrown up, handkerchiefs waved, and a succession of cheers rent the air.

The King's face brightened with a ray of hope, the gentlemen of his Court looked overjoyed, and Colonel Hammond, who with Colonel Baskett of Cowes Castle brought up the rear, exchanged uneasy and apprehensive glances.

The King rode away amid universal acclamation, and the people dispersed to their homes. Frances, for it was no other than she who had been the heroine of the day, curtseyed farewell to the King, smiling at him through her tears, and her brothers, after lavishing many caresses upon her for the modest grace with which she had played her part, led her home.

CHAPTER II

"Not all the water in the rough rude sea
Can wash the balm from an anointed king :
The breath of worldly men cannot depose
The deputy elected by the Lord."

Richard II, Act III, Sc. 2.

IT seemed as if the presence of the Royal visitor in the gloomy old Castle of Carisbrook would be likely to make a great change in the village and neighbourhood. Everything appeared to be going on well. Colonel Hammond treated the King with every mark of respect, accompanying him while hunting in the forest of Parkhurst, which was then plentifully stocked with deer, and ordering every thing for his comfort. His Majesty held his Court at the castle, and the gentry of the island were freely admitted to kiss his hand. The inhabitants of Newport, following up the enthusiastic reception with which they had greeted him on the day of his arrival, further promised security to his person and protection from all dangers.

Dr. Russell and Madam Harcourt lost no time in paying their respects to the King. They obtained leave to present themselves at one of his courts, where they were received with marked favour ; for the King, who never forgot a name, nor a gallant action performed in his service, soon discovered how nearly related they were to the brave Arthur Harcourt, who had died fighting for his cause at Naseby. It will easily be imagined how Madam Harcourt's heart beat high with pleasure when she learnt from his own Royal lips that he had always entertained a deep regard for her lost husband, and how, on being told of his final act of self-sacrifice, the King had resolved, whenever his ill fortune would allow him, to befriend his faithful servant's wife and children.

To his gracious inquiries respecting them, Madam Harcourt replied that she had two sons—the elder they had made bold to call after his Majesty,—and one daughter, the little girl who had ventured to tender him a rose as he rode through Newport. When the King heard this he was still further delighted, for the little episode of the flower had touched him deeply.

But, alas! these days of comparative ease and tranquillity for the unfortunate King were not destined to last. On the 17th of November he had addressed a letter to both Houses of Parliament containing proposals for a personal treaty in London, and he anxiously awaited their answer. Days passed by, and then weeks, and none arrived.

Still Colonel Hammond's demeanour did not alter towards him, and to all appearance he was at liberty to go or stay as he liked, and to follow all his usual pursuits; his gentlemen remained in attendance, he continued to hold his little Court, and his favourite chaplain, Dr. Hammond, uncle to the Governor of the castle, was always with him.

Thus Dr. Russell's scheme of fetching his friend had answered in both respects; for the civility of Colonel Hammond to his Royal guest was doubtless chiefly owing to the strict watch kept by his uncle, who, at the slightest alarm of sinister intentions on the Governor's part, was ready to warn the three faithful servants who had attended the King in his flight,—Mr. Ashburnham, Sir John Berkely, and Colonel Legge. They were prepared at any moment, if needful, to plan an escape, which was quite feasible in the apparent liberty of action allowed them; and more than once they urged the

King to fly to France, and make what treaties he liked
from thence, where he would be in safety. But this did
not suit with the King's notions of duty towards his
kingdom, rebellious and turbulent though it was; and,
till urged by the direst necessity, he resolved not to quit
it.

However, his little band of friends felt it all the more
incumbent on them to care for the safety of which he was
himself so careless, and they watched the Governor
narrowly. Madam Harcourt's two sons had been presented to the King, and had been made entirely happy
by the warm praise which he had bestowed upon their
father. The King took an especial fancy to his namesake
Charles, and, on learning that he was a good clerk, often
sent for him to copy the original draughts of his papers.
By these means the feeling of loyalty inherent in Charles
Harcourt's nature increased almost to idolatry; for there
was a charm in the King's manner which it was impossible
to resist, and which won the hearts of all who served
him, while the dignity and fortitude which he displayed
under his manifold adversities, extorted admiration even
from his bitterest enemies.

Meanwhile Dr. Russell, with his friend Dr. Hammond,
laid their plans, and forwarded letters to the Royalists,
urging them to rally round their King. Arthur Harcourt's
acquaintance with the fishermen and sailors stood him
in good stead; for he was employed to find out which
were the best and swiftest fishing-boats, in case they
should be compelled on an emergency to adopt this means
of escape. Arthur soon learnt the names of all the best
boats, which, sailing up the Medina, used to bring the
produce of their fishing excursions to the Newport
market.

Although the King had as yet heard no tidings from
the Parliament, rumours of all kinds were afloat respecting

the course they were about to adopt. In a contemporary newspaper, the *Mercurius Antipragmaticus*, a quaint and prophetic paragraph appeared, to the effect, " that the King being gone, it is good to fear the children's shoes be not made of the same running leather ; and, therefore, the Houses have sent a message to the Earl of Northumberland to have a strict eye over them that they be not stolen away."

At last, however, on the 14th of December, the Parliament passed four resolutions, to be submitted to the King ; and on the 24th, the Commissioners appointed by the two Houses arrived at Carisbrook and presented their petition. On the part of the Lords appeared the Earls of Denbigh, Northumberland, Kent, Rutland, Pembroke, and Salisbury ; and, on the part of the Commons, Messrs. Bulkely, Lisle, R. Goodwin, and Kemp.

His Majesty returned for answer, " He was assured they could not expect a present reply ; but he would take the same into consideration, and give his answer in a few days."

Four days were allowed him ; but on the day following the arrival of the English Commissioners the Scottish Commission came, in all appearance, to protest against the terms proposed by the English Parliament, but covertly with the intention of making such concessions to the King, as would enable him to sign a private treaty of their own, which they had prepared and once before presented to him at Hampton Court. The terms of the English Treaty, proposed to the King by Parliament, are too well known in history to be recapitulated here : they involved the sacrifice alike of the Church, his honour, and his friends, and their rejection must have been foreseen.

Still the four days were days of anxious consultation with his friends, for the King well knew that if he refused the conditions of the English Parliament, he would be

c

made a close prisoner. He summoned his chaplains and his three faithful servants, and a grave deliberation ensued. The Scotch terms were also taken into consideration, they being less objectionable than the English ; the King resolved to sign their Treaty. This was kept a dead secret ; and as the Scottish Commissioners were fearful of being seized and searched, they made up the contract in lead and buried it in a private garden in the island. Dreading, however, the tremendous consequences which must follow upon the King's refusal to sign the English Treaty, his friends once more urged him to escape. Everything was ready ; the Queen had sent a ship, which was now lying in the Southampton Water, and in her letters she conjured him to make use of it while there was yet opportunity. But the King said he would have a care of that time enough, and he must wait until he had delivered his answer.

When the four days had expired, he sent for the English Commissioners, and a scene of intense excitement ensued. King Charles received them surrounded by his little Court. In attendance were his three faithful gentlemen ; his chaplains, Drs. Hammond, Holdworth, and Heywood ; Sir Thomas Herbert, Sir John Oglander, and other loyal gentlemen of the Isle of Wight ; Dr. Russell, by special request of his Majesty ; and in the background stood Charles Harcourt, who had been the King's amanuensis in preparing his reply. The Commissioners entered, first the representatives of the Lords, then the representatives of the Commons. In reply to the King's majestic inclination of the head they made their salutation, and then Lord Denbigh, as spokesman, opened the interview.

" We come, sire, to request your answer to the proposals made by the two Houses of Parliament, your Majesty's faithful servants."

"We thank you," said King Charles, "for your courtesy in giving us time to consider the terms of those proposals which have been submitted to us, and we would desire to know whether you have been empowered by the said Houses of Parliament to alter any substantial part of the message wherewith you have been entrusted ? "

"We have received no such powers," replied Lord Denbigh, coldly, while the rest of the Commissioners exchanged meaning glances. Whereupon his Majesty beckoned to Charles Harcourt, who held the parchment in his hand. Charles advanced and presented it on one knee to the King, who handed it, sealed, to Lord Denbigh and the Commissioners withdrew. After a short lapse of time, however, they returned, and Lord Denbigh once more addressed the King. "Sire, although we have no authority to treat, or do anything but receive your Majesty's answer, yet we are not to be looked upon as common messengers to carry back an answer which we have not seen ; and unless we are presently permitted to see what is entrusted to us, we will not account it an answer, but rather will depart without any."

It was now the turn of the Royalists to look discomposed and the King himself appeared troubled.

"Wherefore are you so importunate to know the answer we send to the Houses of Parliament ? surely it is but a brief period of a day and a half that we ask you to restrain your curiosity : the contents of our reply will not be long secret."

Still this did not by any means appease the Earl of Denbigh and his colleagues ; and they reiterated with some vehemence their former determination, rather to depart without an answer, than to carry one back of the contents of which they were ignorant.

The King seeming to waver, Mr. Ashburnham gave him a beseeching glance, as if to implore him to stand firm, and to let the Commissioners go, as they said, rather than betray his secret.

Then followed a pause of some moments, which was broken by Lord Denbigh, who observed :

" We do but waste our time and that of your Majesty by any further delay. We will return to those that sent us, and inform them that your Majesty deigns not to accept their overtures of peace " ; and he made a move-ment as if to depart.

One of the chaplains now bent forward and whispered something to the King, who, conceiving that their return without his answer would be attended with the worst consequences, told them that he had some reason for having offered to deliver it to them in that manner, but if they would give him their word that the communicating it to them should be attended with no prejudice to him, he would give it and cause it to be read.

A look of blank dismay spread itself over the counten-ances of the Royalist party ; but the Commissioners readily undertook what was required of them, and Lord Denbigh handed the packet again to the King, who broke the seal and gave it to one of his chaplains to read.

It was as follows :—

" That his Majesty had always thought it a matter of great difficulty to comply in such a manner with all engaged interests, that a firm and lasting peace might ensue : in which opinion he was now confirmed, since the Commissioners from Scotland do solemnly protest against the several Bills and propositions which the two Houses of Parliament had presented to him for his assent ; so that it was not possible for him to give such an answer as might be the foundation of a hopeful peace."

He then proceeded to give them many unanswerable reasons why he could not pass the four Bills as they were offered him, " which did not only divest him of all sovereignty, and leave him without any possibility of recovering it to him or his successors, but opened a door for all intolerable oppressions upon his subjects, he granting such an arbitrary and illimited power to the two Houses." And further, he added these memorable words : " That neither the desire of being freed from that tedious and irksome condition of life, which he had so long suffered, nor the apprehension of anything that might befall him, should ever prevail with him to consent to any one act, till the conditions of the whole peace should be concluded, and then he would be ready to give all just and reasonable satisfaction in all particulars ; and for the adjusting of all this, he knew no way but a personal treaty, and therefore very earnestly desired the two Houses to consent to it, to be either at London, or any other place they would rather choose."*

His Majesty then delivered his reply to the Commissioners, who no sooner received it, than they kissed his hand and departed for Westminster.

The Royalists, who had narrowly watched the countenances of the Commissioners while the King's answer was being read, had observed that they clouded over with displeasure and disappointment at each successive clause, and now that they were gone, the King's friends hastened to communicate their fears to him, lest any alteration of the treatment he had hitherto received at the hands of Colonel Hammond should be the fault of this reply to the Parliament being made known.

His three gentlemen in attendance were urgent that he should lose no time in making his escape ; and implored him that very afternoon to propose a ride to Parkhurst, whence they could easily escape to Cowes, and so to the Queen's vessel which was awaiting him. The King was not ill-disposed to attend to their advice, and

* See Clarendon's *History of the Rebellion*, Vol. V, p. 89.

busied himself in making what preparations were necessary, with regard to his private papers and other matters
of importance.   Meanwhile his gentlemen began eagerly
discussing the mode of escape : through Mr. Ashburnham's care, swift horses were in readiness, the only
question that remained to be considered was, whether the
wind was favourable.   One of them went to the window
to observe the weathercock,—alas ! the wind had veered
since the morning ; and while they were relating this evil
mishap to his Majesty, suddenly, without any previous
notice, Colonel Hammond opened the door and entered
the presence-chamber.   The Royalists, by common consent, grouped themselves round the King, with their
hands on their swords, to defend him from danger, for
they saw that in the Governor's countenance which
boded their master no good.

Unhappily, their fears were destined soon to be realised ;
for Colonel Hammond, in reply to the King's look of
astonishment at being thus suddenly invaded in his
private apartment, muttered forth some faint apology,
and then added, that he was sorry to acquaint his
Majesty with the positive orders that he had received
from his superiors, to forbid Mr. Ashburnham, Colonel
Legge, Sir John Berkely, and the rest of the servants who
were with him at Oxford, any longer to remain in attendance ; and that the jealousies and apprehensions of the
time rendered it incumbent on him to dismiss them from
the castle.

On hearing this, the King's countenance evinced a
great deal of surprise and trouble, and he observed to his
gentlemen that this was an announcement he certainly
did not expect.   Then, turning to Colonel Hammond,
" Why do you use me thus ?   Where are your orders for
it ?   Is it by order of the Commissioners ? "

Hammond replied in the negative ; but added that

he had an order from the Parliament to do as he had done, and that he saw plainly by the King's answer to the propositions of the two Houses, that he acted by other counsels than stood with the good of the kingdom.

" This is too much," said Sir John Berkely, " this insolence in his Majesty's very presence " ; and he advanced as if to seize upon the Governor, who quailed beneath his eye.

" Forbear ! " said the King to Berkely ; " violence will not avail us here." And again addressing Hammond, " Did you not engage your honour you would take no advantage against me if I took shelter in this castle ? "

" I said nothing that might be so construed," replied the Governor.

" You are an equivocating gentleman," said King Charles. " I am destined to learn by bitter experience that mere words are but a frail security for protection, even though they be those of a man who calls himself a man of honour. Leave me now," and he motioned to Colonel Hammond to depart ; " unless, indeed, privacy in my apartment is also denied me."

Colonel Hammond, casting a doubting glance at the Royalist party, dared not demur, and reluctantly retired.

CHAPTER III

" With my own power my majesty they wound ;
In the King's name the King himself's uncrowned :
So doth the dust destroy the diamond."

Poem of *Majesty in Misery*, by King Charles I.

" It is evident," said the King, when he felt assured the
Governor was out of earshot, " that there is no more
confidence to be placed in Colonel Hammond ; perhaps
I did unwisely in ever committing myself to his trust, but
of that matter it is in vain now to discourse. Let us
rather employ our energies in effecting my own speedy
enlargement, and in enlisting the sympathies of all those
who are attached to our cause."

A grave consultation then took place, in which it was
resolved that it was useless to contend against the order
of Parliament respecting his Majesty's gentlemen ; but
that, on the contrary, it would disarm suspicion to let
them depart unhesitatingly while their liberty was yet
allowed them, that they might busy themselves in forwarding the King's escape. They were to seek to gain
adherents to the Royal cause, to keep up a constant
correspondence with the King, and not to leave the
island, unless driven by necessity to do so.

It being understood that the Royal chaplains were to
be also dismissed, Dr. Russell offered to serve in that
capacity if permitted by the Governor, and Charles
Harcourt would continue in his office as secretary, and so
keep up a communication with the Royalist party. This
Dr. Russell felt confident would be allowed, whatever else

was prohibited, on account of his grandson's youth and modest, unobtrusive demeanour. A cipher was agreed upon in which to carry on their correspondence, and all sought to dispel the gloom by the prospect of a speedy release.

On the following day, after the King rose from his dinner, his three faithful gentlemen threw themselves at his feet, and prayed God for his preservation, and then, kissing his hand, departed.

When they were gone, his Majesty, filled with fearful apprehensions, resolved to make one more effort to retain his chaplains. He sent for Colonel Hammond, and remonstrated with him.

" Will you allow me any chaplains ? " he said ; " you pretend for liberty of conscience, shall I have none ? "

" I cannot allow you a chaplain," replied Hammond.

" Shall I have liberty to go about to take the air ? "

" No, I cannot grant it."

The King then charged him with his allegiance, and told him he must answer this.

Dr. Russell, on learning the Governor's refusal respecting the chaplain, besought him to grant him an interview. This would not have been accorded had not Colonel Hammond wished to keep on good terms with Madam Harcourt's father, as the only means of renewing his intimacy with her. He had never forgotten his first attachment, although, partly from mortification, partly from a regard to his own interest, he had married Hampden's daughter. She had been dead some years, and he was again free, and in a position of wealth and importance. The brief glimpse which he had caught of Alice Harcourt as he stood on her father's doorstep had reawakened all the feelings which, though slumbering, had never ceased to exist in his heart. He was aware that the course which he had adopted in the late war would not be likely

to be approved of by her. But now here was an opportunity for him. Was not the King, the centre of all the
fondest hopes and passionate yearnings of the Royalist
party, in his power ? Surely this must influence Alice
Harcourt in his favour, and, in order to help the King,
might she not be induced to relent towards himself ? In
that case should he favour the Royalist schemes ? if not
actively, at all events by remaining passive ? He would
not answer that last question even to himself, but at last
he determined inwardly he would be no party to any
designs upon the King's life, such as had been contem-
plated when his Majesty was imprisoned at Hampton
Court. In this frame of mind he sent word to Dr. Russell
that he would receive him in his private room at the
castle.

The beginning of the interview was far from promising.
Colonel Hammond, in his perplexity, rushed at once into
the subject, lest his confusion should be perceived ; some
dim notion also was floating in his mind that any favour
he might grant would be enhanced if he appeared hard
and inflexible at first.

"I am glad to see you, Dr. Russell," he began,
hurriedly ; "for I wish to tell you that in compliance
with my superior orders, I cannot allow you to attend
upon King Charles any longer. If he stands in need of
spiritual advice there is Mr. Troughton, the chaplain to
the Governor and garrison of the castle ; also Mr. Sedgwick, a famous preacher in the Parliamentarian army,
who is come to this island for the express purpose of discoursing to the King upon his spiritual concernment.
And for your grandson, Charles Harcourt, he comes too
often in and out of the castle ; I cannot have him here
prying and playing the spy."

Dr. Russell listened in silence to this speech, which was
delivered in the would-be defiant tone of a man who felt

he was doing an unjust and tyrannical action, and was ashamed of it. At length he said :

" But a little while ago, Colonel Hammond, you came to me in great distress of mind to implore my advice, and you swore eternal gratitude to me if I would help you out of your difficulty. Methinks all that is forgotten now."

Hammond perceived he had overshot his mark, and said, in an altered tone :

" With respect to the attendance of the chaplains upon the King my orders are strict and must be obeyed ; but as far as this stripling is concerned, my own discretion is my guide, and I know of no reason why I should forbid him the castle, if it pleasure his Majesty, and more especially if you think it would advance me one step on the road to your daughter's favour."

He dropped his voice and averted his face when he came to these last words.

" I can make no promises, nor can I agree to any conditions, and I can give you no hopes of succeeding where you most wish to succeed. I should be deceiving you were I to tell you otherwise. This much, however, I may safely affirm, that my daughter is a devoted Royalist, and that no one need ever hope for her favour who does anything displeasing to the King. I would rather, however, you were guided by your own sense of what is right and honourable, than by any consideration of this kind."

" People's opinions, in these days, differ very much as to what is right," said the Governor, haughtily.

" There are, unhappily, many diversities of opinion upon this point," said Dr. Russell ; " still, matters must be even worse than I imagine if a gentleman's word of honour is no longer any security for the worthy and honourable treatment of the person who trusts to it."

" I mean not to harm his Majesty," said Colonel

Hammond, hastily; "it is for his own good that, by order of my superiors, I have dismissed his gentlemen, who were perpetually poisoning his ear with flattery; and for the chaplains, who, under cover of the Episcopal Church, introduce Popish——"

"Pardon me for the interruption; as I am a brother priest, I cannot hear the doctrines which they hold traduced. But what avails it to discuss these matters? I see also it is of no use to ask you to permit the King's chaplains to return to the castle, but in their enforced absence I would ask as a favour the privilege of ministering to the King's spiritual wants."

"It deeply grieves me, Dr. Russell," said Hammond, "to be compelled to refuse your request; my orders are strict to allow no ordained minister access to King Charles. Be content that I allow your grandson to serve him as secretary ;—that I grant you as an especial favour, for the strictness of my orders scarcely admits of it."

Dr. Russell, perceiving that nothing more was to be gained, and fearing the loss of the small favour already granted, thought it wise to abstain from asking permission even to take leave of the King. "I will not defy you any longer," he said, and withdrew from the Governor's chamber.

Slowly and thoughtfully he descended the hill from the castle, and went at once to the house of his daughter. He found her alone.

"Alice," he said, gravely, "you were quite right; Robert Hammond is not to be trusted. He has evidently received stringent orders from Parliament, and he is not a man to risk his own interest. The King is in his power, alone and unprotected, and dark forebodings fill my mind as to what his fate may be unless we can speedily effect his deliverance."

He then related to his daughter the substance of his

conversation with the Governor. Madam Harcourt listened with a grave countenance.

"Father," she said, " I am sincerely glad you made no conditions and no promises, for I never can fulfil them. If the knowledge of my own personal feelings of loyalty can avail aught to procure for the King treatment befitting his Majesty at the hands of Colonel Hammond, I can but rejoice that it should have that effect, while I deplore deeply that such an incentive should be needed. But further I will not go. We will not take him into our counsels, or with any offer of a bribe obtain his assistance ; it would be wrong to allure him with the prospect of false hopes : such help would not prosper us. Besides, we have the additional reason of knowing that he is unsafe and untrustworthy. The difficulty of our task, I foresee, will be very great ; and I agree with you that we must lose no opportunity, and exert our best efforts to accomplish it. The free access of Charles to the castle will be of vital consequence. The King already seems to place the most perfect trust in him."

" Where is he now ? " asked Dr. Russell.

" He went to Newport about two hours ago with some papers from the King, carefully concealed. I expect him back every minute " ; and she looked towards the window.

" There he comes," she exclaimed, " with Arthur ; but, in heaven's name, what can have happened ? he looks as if he has seen a ghost."

The boys came in together with Frances, who had joined them in the garden.

" O mother ! " said Charles, and he could scarcely speak for agitation, " you remember gallant Captain Burley, our father's friend who fought with him at Naseby ; they have taken him prisoner, and they say he will be hanged as a traitor."

" Cowardly ruffians ! " put in Arthur ; " ever so little more courage, and we could have rescued the King, and sent the Roundheads to the right about."

" Tell us quietly what has happened," said Dr. Russell, for Madam Harcourt was too much overcome to speak.

" It seems," said Charles, making a strong effort to command himself, " that when Mr. Ashburnham, Sir John Berkely, and Colonel Legge, had taken leave of the King, they went to Newport, and they had not been there long when they heard a drum beat ; crowds assembled in the streets, and they became aware that Captain Burley and various others, having heard of the dismissal by the Parliament of the Royal attendants, and of the tyranny exercised towards the King, had risen to rescue him from Carisbrook. The people were so irritated by this injustice and tyranny, that they induced Captain Burley to believe their resentment to have deeper root than it really had, and, causing the drum to be beaten, he urged them, with the rallying cry ' For God, King Charles, and the people,' to seize upon the castle, and set the King at liberty. Unfortunately, although the people had been ready enough with their indignant and pitying words, when it came to the point they seemed to feel it would be too dangerous an enterprise for them to embark in, opposed as they would be by regular troops, so I grieve to say he was only joined by a very few of the townspeople, and the entire muster, of which women and children formed a large part, had but one musket between them. On the summons of the mayor, the military were sent from Carisbrook, and Captain Burley has been committed to prison. O mother ! he looked so noble as he went down the street ; they had bound his hands, and he was closely guarded ; there were one or two others taken with him, but I heard that he only would have to pay for his gallant effort with his life. There were

murmurs in the crowd of ' Shame ! shame ! ' as he passed
along."

" Yes," said Arthur, " and if they had stood by him,
he would not have been in that plight. Oh, if we had
been men, Charles and I, would we not have tried to
rescue our father's friend ! "

" My dear boys, listen to me," said Dr. Russell ; " the
time is coming when you may be of use to the King,
perhaps not in the direct way of fighting for him," and
he smiled sadly, " as you, Arthur, wish so much. Alas !
we must learn from the sad fate of gallant Burley, that
the strength is on the side of the wicked. I fear his life
will be the forfeit of his noble though ill-considered
attempt ; there is no mercy to be hoped for at the hands
of these men—if they show none towards the master,
they will certainly show none towards his servants ; but
we must deliver the King from his imprisonment before
it is too late, and for this great prudence and determination are required, for his enemies have spies in every
direction." He then explained to Charles how Colonel
Hammond would allow him as a great favour to continue
to serve the King as secretary. " Much, therefore," he
said, " will depend upon you ; you must be quiet and
discreet, watch narrowly the conduct of the Governor,
and carefully conceal from him any papers committed to
your trust. I need not remind you what a great privilege
has fallen to your share in being thus permitted to attend
upon his Majesty, and I have no fear but that, like your
father before you, you will prove true to the Harcourt
motto."

" That I will, grandfather," said Charles, his face
flushed with excitement.

" And you, Arthur," continued Dr. Russell, " can also
be of great service. A boat will soon be required to convey
the King on board ship out of reach of his enemies, so

keep up a close connection with the fishermen, and when you have found one that you can rely upon, reveal to him that his services will be needed to convey an unfortunate Cavalier out of the country; don't disclose who the person really is until the very last, and not then unless absolutely necessary."

Dr. Russell then asked Charles if he had brought back any papers for the King from Newport. Charles replied that the noise and confusion in the crowd had been so great that he had feared to take his Majesty's letters to the post-office, lest he should excite suspicion, and the letters be seized, which would have led to great mischief. He purposed to make another endeavour to-morrow, when the town would be quiet, and it was therefore agreed that Charles had better defer his visit to the castle till the next day, when he might have some certain intelligence to carry to the King. Perceiving how sad and anxious his daughter looked, Dr. Russell stayed some time with her trying to soothe and comfort her. The news of Captain Burley's arrest had been a great shock to her, for his name had vividly recalled the past. Her husband had often spoken of him, and it was Captain Burley who, on his return to the Isle of Wight, after the breaking up of the Royal army, had brought her a few details of her husband's last hours of life, and his dying messages to her. No wonder, then, if the prospect of the sad fate of this faithful friend overwhelmed her with horror and grief. On the following day, when Charles returned from Newport early in the afternoon, he had news of importance to communicate. It appeared that, as he was making his way to the post-office with the packet of letters entrusted to him, a beggar asked alms of him, and on Charles producing a small coin stamped with the King's head, the beggar, pointing to the image, said, " God save him ! "

TRIAL OF KING CHARLES I.

AFTER W. FISK.

facing p. 48.

" Amen ! " Charles replied.

" Follow me," pursued the beggar, " if you are a true servant of the King, before you commit the packet of letters which I know you carry to the post-office ; three gentlemen," and he drew the initials on the ground with his crutch, A., B., and L., " sent me here to watch for you."

Charles followed him cautiously down a back street into a small house, where he unlocked the door and entered, shutting it carefully behind him. There was no one in the room.

" You have heard of Major Bosville," said the beggar ; " I am he," and he pulled off his tattered hat and ragged coat ; " and you are Charles Harcourt, by the description that has been given me of you. I come from Netley Castle, where the Royalists are, having been forced to fly from the island, and I am here for two reasons. Firstly, because we have discovered that Witherings, of the post-office, is not to be trusted, so do not commit any more of the King's packets to his care. And, secondly, to tell you how we have secured a loyal servant who will, we think, be placed in immediate attendance upon his Majesty. His name is Firebrace ; he was a former dependent of the King, and he has now received from Mr. Ashburnham an order to hasten to the castle with what intelligence of the Royalist movements he could procure. In order to gain admittance there, he has feigned a great wish to serve the Parliament, and went to the Speaker to obtain from him a recommendation to Colonel Hammond to make him one of the pages of the Royal bed-chamber. This he has actually got, and it is of the greatest consequence ; but we are very anxious that the King should be told of this, lest he should manifest joy at seeing his old servant, and thus defeat the whole scheme. You must, therefore, contrive to tell the King

D

before Firebrace's arrival at the castle, which will be either this afternoon or to-morrow morning. I tried to find you yesterday, and waited for you a long while, till the hubbub increased so in the town that I was forced to leave it for fear of being discovered and sent to prison."

Major Bosville then asked Charles to give him the packet of letters, promising to take them to Netley Castle, whence they would be forwarded. Perceiving that Charles still hesitated, he pulled from his pocket a copy of the cipher employed by the King and proceeded to decipher it.

" Then," said Charles, in conclusion, " I thought it wrong to doubt any more, so I delivered the packet to his charge, and I must lose no time in telling the King."

It was about an hour before his Majesty's usual time for dining, when Charles Harcourt arrived at the castle. He entered without difficulty, Colonel Hammond having given orders for his immediate admission within the walls ; but, as he was about to proceed to the Royal apartments, a firm hand grasped his shoulder.

" Not so fast, young man," said a voice behind him ; " I will accompany you " ; and no less a person than the Governor himself ushered him into the presence-chamber.

King Charles was busily engaged in writing, which occupied a large portion of his time. On hearing them enter, he paused and looked up, then held out his hand to Charles, who advanced, knelt on one knee and kissed it. Colonel Hammond remained in the room.

" I am glad to see you," said the King to his secretary, with a gracious smile, " for I have some copying for you to do," and he handed him some sheets of paper closely written, which he held up so that the Governor might have a full view of them. " They are some notes that we have taken at different times from Hooker's *Ecclesiastical Polity;* our library is circumscribed, and we must rather perfect our acquaintance with the books at our command, than seek to extend our information."

" Your Majesty's time seems well filled with the study of those you possess, to judge from the notes taken in writing, which appear to be extremely copious," observed the Governor, ironically.

The King, who understood the real meaning disguised under this remark, replied with dignity : " If, in compliance with your orders, you think it necessary to watch narrowly our recreation and daily exercise, methinks we might at least claim the right of privacy during those hours which we devote to study."

Colonel Hammond, perceiving the indignant flush which his impertinence had called up in young Harcourt's face, muttered something about it being his duty to see his Majesty's health was not injured by so much reading, and, after an awkward pause, went away. For the first few minutes after he was gone the silence continued.

The King sat motionless, shading his face with his hands. His countenance wore an expression of profound melancholy, as he gazed fixedly through the narrow window of his apartment. Alas ! it was only too evident that he was in a prison hard to escape from. The rooms which he occupied were in the centre of the castle—the Salisbury Tower, as it was called. They were all on the first floor, the view was confined by the battlements, and in spite of the elevated situation of the castle, nothing much beyond the bowling green, where the King was wont to walk and sit on fine evenings, as the summer advanced, was discernible. At length he said, with some bitterness, " I would the Governor's feigned care for my health took the form of inducing him to vary my recreation, and of allowing me to resume my rides, instead of cavilling at my only means of passing these weary hours of my captivity," and he sighed.

" I trust, Sire," said Charles, looking up from his writing, " your deliverence from this irksome prison will not be much longer delayed."

The King gave him an inquiring glance, and his secretary, having first examined carefully the hangings of the room, to see if any one was concealed there, opened the door gently, and perceiving that all was safe, related to his Majesty what Major Bosville had told him that morning. The King was overjoyed at hearing of Firebrace's probable arrival at the castle—it was a fresh gleam of hope ; also of the efforts made for his deliverance by the Royalists at Netley Castle, and how, although within the walls of his prison he was so closely guarded, friends devoted to his service nightly hovered on the sea-shores and watched about his dwelling. Charles Harcourt, fearful lest he should give him pain, did not mention the fate of Captain Burley, but presently the King observed : " About noon yesterday I noticed a great stir going on in the castle, and a troop of soldiers were dispatched in the direction of Newport. I asked the Governor the cause of this, and he replied, in a somewhat confused manner, that there had been an uproar in the town, and that the mayor had sent for the military to restore order. Did you see anything of it when you were in Newport ? " Thus pressed, Charles narrated as concisely as he could what had occurred, dwelling upon the gallant conduct of Captain Burley. When he ceased, the King covered his face with his hands. " Alas ! " he said, " I am doomed to bring ruin and death upon all who espouse my unhappy cause ; my gallant friends, one by one, they perish in the attempt to save me. Perhaps I had better yield before more noble lives are forfeited on my account. But that treaty : I can never sign that, and nothing less will satisfy them. Rather let them take my life than my honour."

" Sire," cried Charles, and, starting up, he threw himself on his knees at his master's feet, while he seized one of his hands and passionately kissed it, " there is not one of us who would no. sooner die twenty times, if such were possible, rather than leave untried a single means to deliver you from this prison and set you again on your rightful throne. My life, poor and worthless as it is, is at your service, and if it is God's will that I should perish in the attempt, I should feel it only too great happiness to die in so noble a cause."

" My brave boy, my namesake," said the King, smiling sadly, as he passed his hand over the boy's head, " I trust in God my liberty will not be purchased at the cost of your bright young life ; but if ever it should please Him to restore me to the throne of my father, I will not forget any one of the generous efforts which have been made to help me in my adversity." Hearing footsteps in the passage, young Harcourt rose to his feet, and resumed his writing. The Governor entered. " A new attendant," he said, " one Firebrace by name, sent by the Speaker of the House of Commons, has just arrived. He claims to be made page of the Royal bed-chamber, if it be agreeable to your Majesty."

" I have no choice in these matters," said the King, without looking up from the book he was reading, " and of what avails it to mock me with the pretence of it ? "

" Will it please your Majesty to see him now, or at the usual hour of dinner, when he will be in attendance ? " persisted the Governor.

" I will see him then, I do not wish to be disturbed now " ; and the King still continued to read. Colonel Hammond, however, remained in the Royal presence, till at last Charles Harcourt guessed why he was waiting, and rose to ask the King the meaning of a word which he could not decipher ; their eyes met, and Charles gave a meaning

look towards the door, whereupon the King said to him :
" You may retire now ; if you have any leisure moments
which you can devote towards making a fair copy of
those crabbed notes, either to-morrow or next day, I
shall be glad of your services."

" My time is always at your Majesty's disposal,"
replied Charles, and he withdrew. Colonel Hammond
accompanied him out of the Royal suite of apartments,
watching him narrowly, lest he should speak to any of
the guards. The Governor was already half inclined to
repent that he had given young Harcourt leave to attend
in this way upon the King, and he perceived that many
difficulties might arise in consequence.

He was still undecided as to the line of conduct which
he should adopt towards his Royal prisoner, and he felt
that Charles Harcourt might be an inconvenient spy
upon him ; yet, on the other hand, he reflected that if he
were now to dismiss the lad from the castle, he would
thereby forfeit any chance of being allowed to renew the
friendly intercourse with Madam Harcourt which he had
so much desired. Even as matters stood this was difficult
enough, and he was at a loss how to begin. The responsible nature of his office scarcely admitted of his
leaving the castle, and had it been otherwise, he had not
courage to seek her out and endeavour to renew his
acquaintance with her, for he knew well the quiet determination of her character, and he felt that if he were too
precipitate he would run the risk of being for ever for-
bidden her presence. So he was forced to content himself
with now and then asking Charles, in a half shy, half
defiant tone, " how his mother did," and he would beg
to be remembered to her ; but as no message was ever
brought to him in return, he discontinued even this
ordinary civility. Still, Charles continued his attendance
as secretary, and secretly was the medium of a corre-

spondence between the King and his friends, and thus passed the two first months of his Majesty's captivity. March had now begun, and the Royalists, who had been actively engaged in devising a scheme for his deliverance, felt no more time was to be lost. They were only waiting to know how far the King's personal attendants were to be trusted before they made the attempt.

One day when young Charles, accompanied by the Governor, having left the presence-chamber, was making his way past the sentinels stationed at the several doors of the Royal suite of apartments, just as he was reaching the last, a loud angry discussion behind them caused Colonel Hammond hastily to turn his head, and the sentinel close to Charles seized the opportunity to slip a paper into his hand, which young Harcourt quickly concealed, and did not open till he reached his own home.

CHAPTER IV

" For loyalty is still the same
Whether it win or lose the game :
True as the dial to the sun,
Although it be not shined upon."
Hudibras, Part III, Canto 2.

" HE was the worthiest gentleman, the best master, the best friend, the best husband, the best father, and the best Christian that the age in which he lived produced."

Such is the well-known eulogy of King Charles by the great contemporary historian, Clarendon, after a careful summary, in which the King's merits are accurately weighed, and his claims alike upon our sympathy and admiration elaborately set forth. We are the more ready to believe in the truth and justice of these statements because the same historian does not allow himself to be blinded by his feelings of loyalty to the faults of his sovereign.

Perhaps a yet more powerful testimony to the lovableness and goodness of the King's character is to be found in the devoted attachment displayed by his friends throughout his adverse fortunes, and the deeply-rooted loyalty of his followers never appears to more advantage than during his imprisonment in the Isle of Wight, when he was destitute of means to bribe the sordid or excite the ambitious.

A deep tinge of romance colours this epoch of King Charles's history, and sad memories of his lonely captivity, only varied by the fruitless efforts of his friends to set

56

him free, are for ever associated with the grey and gloomy walls of Carisbrook Castle.

To return to our story.   When safe in his own room, Charles Harcourt unfolded the piece of paper which had been given him by the sentinel at the castle.   On it were written these words :—

" I am the King's gentleman-usher. I wish to help him, and forward his escape, for I know him to be in unsafe quarters here, in the hands of traitors.   The Governor believes me to be the servant of the Parliament, and placed me in attendance as a spy, but he reckons without his host.   When you pass by next I will have one glove off, that you may recognise me.   Dowcett, the other attendant, is faithful to the King, and knows Firebrace.   Be vigilant, and tell the King's friends abroad *to lose no time.*   ·   " OSBORNE."

Charles Harcourt communicated this valuable intelligence at once to his grandfather, and it was agreed, when they all were assembled that evening in family conclave, that Dr. Russell should proceed on the following day to Netley Castle to apprise the Royalists of the favourable aspect of affairs at Carisbrook, in order that his Majesty's escape might be effected speedily, lest the ever-watchful suspicions of the Governor should be aroused, and a change be made in the Royal attendants.   Arthur was to accompany his grandfather, in order to find out when and where the fishing-boat was to be in readiness to convey the King to the vessel awaiting him, or to the opposite shore, as the case might be.

Charles spent that day with his mother and sister, and he found great relief in discussing with them the subject which they all had so much at heart.

Madam Harcourt's good sense and excellent judgment were of inestimable value, enabling her to make many wise suggestions in the arrangement of the scheme for the King's escape.

" If the Royal attendants can be won over to his Majesty's side," she said, " it seems to me that other difficulties would be as nothing. How many of them do you say there are ? "

Her son began to enumerate.

" I think, as far as I can learn, there are only thirty persons allowed within the walls of the castle as servants to the King. Of these, four gentlemen have been selected to wait and watch by turns two and two at the door of his apartment by day, when he is within it, and at the entrance of his chamber by night, against which their beds are closely drawn so as to prevent all means of ingress or egress till removed in the morning. These gentlemen have been approved by the committee of the House of Commons at Derby House ; they are Mr. Herbert, Mr. Mildmay, Mr. Preston, and Captain Silas Titus. I know nothing of them as yet, except indeed Captain Titus by sight, because I heard the Governor address him by his name when I was there yesterday : he is a young man of about five-and-twenty, with a brave, honest countenance. I do not know why, but I felt confidence in him directly I saw him. Then there is Mr. Osborne, the King's gentleman-usher, and his office is to hold his Majesty's glove during dinner. Dowcett and Firebrace are pages of the Royal bed-chamber. Firebrace we know to be faithful, and Mr. Osborne seems, by his letter, to have won Dowcett over to the King's side. There are also the laundress, Mrs. Wheeler, and her assistant. I do not know any others of the household."

" But, brother," said Frances, who had been listening attentively to this narration, " if Mrs. Wheeler is faithful and to be trusted, and if all other means fail, would it not be a good thing to communicate with his

Majesty by introducing letters between the folds of his linen ? "

" It would be a very good plan," said Charles ; " it had never occurred to me. We must, however, first find out if Mrs. Wheeler is to be depended on, and then if we are driven to great straits we can employ it ; only, of course, the fewer people we trust with a secret the more likely it is to be kept."

" And now tell me, Charles," said Madam Harcourt, " a little about his Majesty's apartments : are they at all spacious ? do they mock him with the appearance of being lodged in a palace, or do they not disguise the fact that he is in reality confined in a prison ? "

" There is little of both, mother, although the appearance of the one is meant to conceal the reality of the other. The room—the presence-chamber, as it is called—is long and narrow, badly lit by one small window at the end ; the walls are hung with arras hangings, and the crimson and yellow damask curtains but ill conceal the massive iron bars which guard the window. Then there is a great show of chairs and footstools of green velvet, and a piece of Turkey carpet covers the floor ; but I think his Majesty would willingly exchange all this state for a little more variety in his recreation and the permission to ride again. I fear it is in vain to hope for this until he is delivered from his prison. Only the other day I heard Colonel Hammond remonstrating with him for walking so fast when he was taking his allotted exercise within the castle walls."

" No ! " said Madam Harcourt ; " he did not really dare do that ! "

" He did, indeed," continued Charles ; " and you know the King always likes to walk very fast with a cane. At last I heard him tell the Governor, in a pointed manner, that that was the last ' argumentation ' he would hold

with him about it. It makes my blood boil to think that
such a man as that has it in his power to vex and harass
the King in the way he does ; if he had made the smallest
effort to alleviate the weariness and abate the rigours of
his captivity, there would be something to be said in his
favour ; but as it is, he first lured the King with a promise
of protection and security, and now, utterly regardless of
his plighted word, he not only keeps him a captive, but
never ceases to annoy him with petty regulations and
unnecessary restraints. Indeed," he added, in a lower
voice, " I never feel certain that he may not be worked
upon by bribes to make an attempt against the life of his
sacred Majesty."

Frances ceased turning her spinning-wheel, and looked
at her brother with an expression of horror upon her face ;
while Madam Harcourt said, " Oh, hush, Charles ! God
forbid that any such wicked thought should enter into
his head ! It cannot be ; besides, even for their own
sakes, it would never answer the wicked ends of his
employers to urge him to commit so foul a crime. They
would be held in universal execration throughout the
world ; but do not let us think of it, much less talk of
it."

" My dear mother," said Charles, " I am sorry if I have
said aught to distress you. I had no right to impart to
you my own forebodings ; rather let us hope that we may
defeat their purposes entirely by rescuing the King from
his captivity. Frances, shall we take a walk to the foot
of the castle steep, to pass the time until grandfather
and Arthur return ? Mother, dear, do come too, you
look so pale and anxious, some fresh air will do you
good."

Madam Harcourt yielded to her son's entreaties, and
all three went out together. The afternoon was bright
and sunny, and there was a softness in the air announcing

the approach of spring. Already the violets were beginning to show themselves in the hedgerows; and
Frances, who loved flowers, began eagerly to gather them
as they went along their favourite walk to Carisbrook
Church. It was a very old building, in the Norman style
of architecture, and it stood on a slight elevation, answering to the opposite side, which was crowned by the stern
and gloomy castle. Although the actual fabric of the
church had, in its ancient solidity, withstood the rude
assaults of the Puritans, within were broken windows
and images, tombs defaced, and the pavement torn up.
No one durst enter it now to pray there, for fear of being
seized as a Malignant, and the unfrequented, grass-grown
paths bore witness to its entire desertion. Yet Madam
Harcourt, in spite of its melancholy aspect, loved to
wander near the church where her father had for so many
years officiated as priest and ministered to the wants of
many a weary soul.

"Alas!" she thought, "and will it always be thus?
Is the voice of the Church silenced for ever while the
houses of God throughout the land are dismantled, even
like this one, or entirely destroyed; her bishops and
priests are hunted from their benefices, and the King,
because he will not sanction all this, is shut up in a prison.
How long, O Lord! how long?"

She was aroused from her reverie by Charles. "Look,
mother," he said, as he pointed to a woman with a yoke
and two pails coming down the hill; "that is Mrs.
Wheeler—I suppose she is coming to the brook for water,
though why she should come down here, when there is
that famous well at the castle, I am at a loss to imagine.
Let us wait and ask if she knows how his Majesty does
to-day."

The woman approached: she was about the middle
height, handsome, with a bright, healthy complexion,

and a pleasant smile. When she saw Madam Harcourt and her children she made a low curtsey.

" Good evening, madam," she said ; " and, asking your pardon, sir, be you the young gentleman as writes for his Majesty the King ? "

Charles, somewhat surprised at being thus suddenly addressed, replied that he was, for the present, the King's secretary.

Mrs. Wheeler went on : " I thought as much ; for I saw you pass once or twice when I was washing in the laundry." And then, looking cautiously round, she added, in a lower tone of voice, " You would be glad to get him out of that mopy old prison," indicating the castle with her thumb, " wouldn't you ? Nay, never fear me, I am as true as steel ; and I wish his Majesty were back on his throne, where he has every right to be. I came down to this brook for water, on purpose to find you and tell you that you might count upon me. The soldiers asked me where I was going with my pails, when there was the well at hand ; but I told them the donkey was out at pasture, and no one could draw me a pailful : besides, it isn't fit water to use for his Majesty's lace."

She ceased from want of breath, and Madam Harcourt thought it was time now to interpose. " We are indeed glad to hear that you, too, will help us, Mrs. Wheeler," she said ; " for we shall need all the assistance we can get. But I am sure you will readily understand that the utmost caution and secrecy will be required, lest, if we fail, we should bring a still worse fate upon him whom we are so desirous to serve."

Mrs. Wheeler promised to be both careful and discreet, and then went on to say that she was going into the village to seek for a new assistant, her former one having been dismissed ; " and if you've no objection, madam, I'll just step in and see my cousin Nicholas on my way back. I've not seen him to speak to for a long while, and mayhap we two together may hit upon some way of helping the King. If I come about dusk no one will be the wiser for it ; and I reckon their spies have too much to think on to be looking after the like of me."

Madam Harcourt gave her consent, and, repeating her warning as to caution, turned towards home with her children.

As they went along, Frances was silent and thoughtful ; she was revolving a plan in her mind which she could scarcely summon courage to impart to her mother. At length she began in a hesitating voice, as she picked to pieces one of the flowers which she held in her hand, " Dear mother, I should like to ask you something very much, but I fear you will not like it."

" What is it, dear child ? " said Madam Harcourt in a gentle voice.

Thus encouraged, Frances plunged at once into her subject : " I have so often and so earnestly longed to be of use to the King," she said, hurriedly ; " and if it would not be very distasteful to you, I should like to disguise myself as Mrs. Wheeler's laundry assistant, and return with her to the castle. I know enough of her trade not to make any great mistakes, and being on the spot at the castle, I might be of service in taking letters to or from his Majesty."

Madam Harcourt, with all her loyalty, was aghast at this unexpected proposal. She could not bear the thought of her daughter up at the castle, among a garrison of rude soldiers, in the capacity of laundry-maid, where she might be exposed to trials and difficulties of which she was perfectly ignorant.

" But, mother," pleaded Frances, " it would only be for such a little while ; the King will soon be able to make his escape, and then I can come away directly.

I know you will trust me ; Charles—speak for me," she said, piteously.

A great struggle was going on in her brother's mind. He saw all the possible advantages of the scheme, more especially as he was quick enough to observe that the Governor disliked him personally, and might any day put a stop to his attendance at the castle ; so if he were the sole channel of communication between the King and his friends, it might easily be stopped. On the other hand, he could not bear the idea of his delicate, refined sister working as a laundry-maid in a coarse dress, with the additional risk of being, in spite of it, discovered and then imprisoned, to say nothing of the daily and hourly disagreeable circumstances incident to her new position. He knew not what to answer.

" Frances," he said at last, gravely, " have you thought sufficiently of what you wish to undertake ? Have you considered the hardships, trials, and great risks you will incur ? "

" I do not mind anything, if I can only serve the King," said Frances, eagerly. " O mother ! do consider what I have said."

" I will," said Madam Harcourt, " when your grandfather comes back ; but I must wait till I see him before I can say anything decided."

At the close of the day, about dusk, Dr. Russell and Arthur returned bringing with them two Royalist gentlemen from Netley Castle ; one was Mr. Edward Worsley, of Gatcombe, and the other Mr. John Newland, son of the gentleman who had purchased Madam Harcourt's property. John Newland's father was, as has been already said, the intimate friend of Colonel Harcourt, and they had for a while fought together in the same army ; but Mr. Newland had been so badly wounded in a skirmish at the beginning of the war, that he had been obliged to return home, completely disabled. His son John, though only a lad of nineteen, had continued to fight gallantly at the head of the troop sent by his father to support the Royal cause, and did not lay down his arms till the disbanding of the Royal army after the capture of the King. Eager and enthusiastic, in all the pride of his youth and strength, it galled him to the quick to be beaten out of the field by the much-despised Puritans and hated Roundheads; and when all the disastrous efforts of 1647 had culminated in the King's being a prisoner in the hands of a crop-eared cur like Hammond, as he called him, all his passions were roused, and he determined to strain every nerve to set him free. For this purpose he and his friend Worsley had joined themselves closely to the band of Royalists at Netley Castle, who had made the King's freedom the end and object of their lives. No sooner had they heard Dr. Russell's report of the state of affairs at Carisbrook, than they came to the unanimous conclusion that the escape must be effected as soon as possible. It was therefore agreed that John Newland and Edward Worsley should return with Dr. Russell and Arthur, and that it should be their duty to provide horses, to await the King outside the castle, and to keep up a constant communication with him. Now the question that remained to be solved was, how early the King could be made acquainted with their scheme. Firebrace would be the best person to communicate with, as he would have to arrange the most difficult part of the escape within the prison walls; but who was to tell Firebrace?

The Governor did not allow the King's attendants to leave the castle on any pretence whatsoever, and it was, of course, of vital importance that all the details of the escape, the day and precise hour, should be made known to those who were to forward it from outside, as well as to

E

those who were within. Dr. Russell asked Charles whether
he thought it would be possible for him to communicate
with Firebrace. Charles replied that he was always
narrowly watched, but he might succeed in eluding the
Governor's vigilance ; at all events, he would not let
slip any opportunity which might occur. The Royalists
then proceeded to draw up their scheme in a concise form.

The escape, if it suited the King's convenience, was to
be fixed for the twentieth of that month. Mr. Worsley
and Mr. Osborne would wait outside the counterscarp
which was beyond the wall of the castle, with a good
horse, saddle, and boots for the King ; the counterscarp
being low, they would easily manage from their horses
to help his Majesty over the wall. Meanwhile, at the
seaside, in a convenient place, John Newland and Arthur
Harcourt would be ready with a stout boat to convey
the King to what part he thought fit. Firebrace was to
arrange how to conduct the Royal captive from his
chamber to the great wall of the castle. This important
letter was written in cipher, folded and sealed, and it
was about to be fastened inside the lining of Charles
Harcourt's coat, for the better concealment of it, when
there was a knock at the door, and Nicholas entered,
bearing a letter addressed to Dr. Russell. It had been
left at his lodging in the morning, and, believing it to be
important, the servant had brought it to Madam Harcourt's house, knowing Dr. Russell would be likely to go
there first on his return from Southampton. The letter
was from Colonel Hammond, and a look of blank dismay
came over Dr. Russell's face as he perused it.

It was brief, and ran thus :—

" Sir,

    " As I am compelled to be absent from the castle
on matters of importance for two days, and as rumours

have reached me of plots being contrived to set the King at liberty contrary to the wishes of Parliament, I have issued strict orders that no one is to go in or out of the castle during my absence. I cannot, therefore, permit your grandson to attend upon the King as secretary till further intelligence received from me.

" Yours, &c. &c.,
" Robert Hammond.

" Carisbrook Castle,
   " *March* 16, 1648."

And then a postscript, in a very small hand :

" I pray you commend me respectfully to Madam Harcourt."

What was to be done now ? Their only means of communication was thus at an end till an indefinite period, and this at a time when every moment was of the utmost importance. The Royalists looked at each other in dumb despair. Frances then went up to her mother and said, in a low but imploring whisper :

" Do tell them about Mrs. Wheeler, and my plan of being her assistant."

Madam Harcourt saw that for the present scheme this was their only chance ; and, although sorely reluctant when she thought of her daughter's risk, propounded it.

There was an anxious pause, and Dr. Russell looked very grave. Even Arthur, who was scarcely old enough to understand all the danger of the undertaking, was sobered ; and Charles went up to his sister.

" Frances," he said, taking her hand fondly in his, " have you weighed it well—have you considered the risk ? "

Frances looked down, a deep blush rose to her face while she said, modestly :

" I am not afraid ; God will protect me."

At last Edward Worsley spoke :

" Madam Harcourt, if you had not proposed this plan to deliver us out of our present distress, no one else could have done so ; but it appears to me that now on it hangs the whole success of the King's escape.   This attempt cannot be made unless his Majesty is apprised at once. Much danger attends any delay ; his attendants may be changed, or the plot discovered.   Words fail me to say how highly I applaud Mistress Frances for her courage and noble self-sacrifice, and as it is only for four days, I think——."

" Stop, Worsley," said John Newland ; " it cannot be—the risk is too great, the peril too imminent.   Think if she were discovered ; or even if that were averted, think of the hourly uncertainty of her position.   Madam Harcourt," he added, turning to her, " you must not sanction this."

But Frances had possessed herself of her mother's hand, and was imploring her to yield in the most persuasive tones.

" Only four days, mother, and then the King will be safe—think of that ! "

" O father ! " said Madam Harcourt, beseechingly, to Dr. Russell ; " what am I to say ? "

The scene had now become intensely exciting.   Frances, with an impetuosity unlike the usual staid quietness of her demeanour, had left her mother's side, and, running up to her grandfather, had caught his hand, while, with flushed face and eyes brilliant with excitement, she implored him to give his advice in her favour.   Charles was engaged in soothing his mother, who could scarcely restrain her agitation, and John Newland walked up and down the room, his long sword clanking at every step, now and then pausing to cast a look of admiration upon Frances in her pretty attitude of pleading.   Edward

Worsley and Arthur were conversing in low tones apart.

Darkness was fast coming on, and as the sun went down a gale arose which now swept in moaning gusts round the house. Thus all the outward circumstances tended to discourage Madam Harcourt as she gazed sadly out of the window, and to disincline her more and more to her daughter's scheme. "Where would Frances be that time to-morrow?" she thought. "Perhaps not even under shelter; certainly not in the comfortable dwelling she had all her life been accustomed to—perhaps doing hard work, amid rude and staring soldiers." But, fortunately for the Royalist hopes, as she reached this point in her meditation, Dr. Russell, gently disengaging himself from Frances, approached and seated himself beside her.

"Alice," he began, "my dear child, it must seem hard to you to be called upon to make another sacrifice in this desperate cause."

"It is not that, father," she said, hastily; "it is the cause only which makes me incline towards it; but oh, if harm were to happen to her, should I have done my duty in permitting this?"

"We must take all reasonable precautions," said Dr. Russell. "Everything seems to me to depend upon whether Mrs. Wheeler is a trustworthy person or not; if this be so, I think she will be able to shield Frances from all those dangers which naturally enough you dread for her. And when one thinks of the probable shortness of the time, and the great benefit which would accrue to him whose cause is so dear to us, I think we are justified in making the venture, provided this courageous little maiden," and he caressed Frances, who had sprung up to kiss him in the intensity of her joy, "feels no shrinking from the task."

" Be it as you say, father," said Madam Harcourt.
" I will not let my weak waverings stand in the way of
your better judgment. Frances, my darling child," and
her voice faltered a little, " may God watch over you ! "

" Amen ! " said John Newland, who, on reflection,
had brought himself to view the matter in a more favourable light ; " and I only wish they could find employment
for me also at the castle, that I might be there to protect
Mistress Frances. What think you, Dr. Russell ? shall
I presently disguise myself as one of their Puritan selves,
and go up yonder to offer my services as a soldier of the
garrison ? "

" I think it would be imprudent," said Dr. Russell ;
" Colonel Hammond's suspicions are already aroused,
and it would be only running a needless risk. We know
that several of the attendants and soldiers are faithful
to the King, so there is no absolute necessity for your
doing this, and your services are more likely to be required outside the castle in forwarding the escape, as we
have already arranged in the letter to Firebrace. I think
it will be necessary both for you and Mr. Worsley to
conceal yourselves if you remain here, and you had
better consider what disguise you mean to assume."

While this conversation was going on, Madam Harcourt had retired with Frances, and presently she returned
alone.

" Mrs. Wheeler is here," she said. " I have confided
to her our scheme, and she declares herself willing to
further it in every way, and, not having been able to
find another assistant, there will be no difficulty in the
way of Frances' temporarily discharging that office. She
has promised me she will take care of her ; and she
declares that the garrison and Royal household are kept
under strict discipline by Colonel Hammond—that there
are no drunken brawls, and that everything is conducted

with the even monotony of a jail. She thinks that Frances
will soon find means to communicate with the King, as
she knows that most of the Royal attendants are anxious
to help him out of his captivity. She says, moreover,
that it is too late to go to the Castle to-night, as the gates
are all closed at eight o'clock. To-morrow morning she
will return there with Frances, and that will give us more
time to contrive the necessary disguise. I confess," said
Madam Harcourt, smiling faintly, " I asked Mrs. Wheeler
if she would undertake alone to deliver the letter, supposing you were prevailed upon to trust her with it, but
she firmly declined, saying she durst not do it alone ; but
I am easier now about this matter. I feel I can depend
upon her ; there is a look of genuine honesty in her face,
and her manner was deferential, although I saw she was
full of compassion for my distress. After all, it is only
for four days," said the poor mother ; " to-morrow, and
the next day, and the next, and then I shall have my
darling back."

Dr. Russell was much moved by the great unselfishness
which his daughter had shown, and her entire confidence
in his judgment ; but, fearful of agitating her by saying
any more upon the subject, he only pressed her hand
tenderly, and tried to divert her mind towards other
matters connected with the great design which occupied
all their thoughts.

" How can we conceal these two gentlemen," he said,
" for the next few days, while they complete their preparations ? Unless they adopt some disguise Colonel
Hammond's spies will soon discover who they are ; he is
already only too intimately acquainted with our design,
although heaven send he may not also have discovered
the means by which we are to accomplish it."

Madam Harcourt began to think ; and John Newland
said :

" Madam, if you will employ me as a gardener for a day or two, it would do capitally. Nicholas has as much as he can do in the house ; and if you will let me dig up Mistress Frances' plot of ground and tend the flowers, I will make good use of your permission."

" Certainly, sir," said Madam Harcourt, " and very grateful I should be for your services. Nicholas will contrive you a disguise."

" And I," said Edward Worsley, " will go to my father's house at Gatcombe, where I will disguise myself as groom, and in that capacity will provide horses for the King from my father's stables. I told Mr. Ashburnham I would have a care of that part of the undertaking. Of course, I shall confide in my father and in the old servants of the household—heaven knows there are few of them left now ; but if the neighbours were to find out that Mr. Worsley's Cavalier son was home from the wars, and residing so near his Royal master, Puritan spies would soon leave me no peace, and either clap me into prison, or compel me to leave the island, and there would be an end of my share in this undertaking."

And thus everything was satisfactorily arranged so far as the actors outside the castle were concerned. The more difficult part to be played within the castle walls, by him upon whom all their loyal hopes were fastened, was yet to be contrived.

CHAPTER V

" We are amazed ; and thus long have we stood
To watch the fearful bending of thy knee,
Because we thought ourselves thy lawful King :
And if we be, how dare thy joints forget
To pay their awful duty to our presence ?
If we be not, show us the hand of God
That hath dismissed us from our stewardship."

Richard II, Act III, Sc. 3.

THE departure of Colonel Hammond from Carisbrook
for a few days, mentioned in the last chapter, far from
diminishing, only increased the restraints which were
already put upon the King's liberty. The responsible
nature of his charge so oppressed the Governor, that he
resolved if possible to rid himself of it by obtaining the
removal of the King. He was weary of the part which
he had to play, in perpetually thwarting one whom, in his
secret heart, he was inclined to respect. He had no well-
defined principles of his own ; secret motives combined
to assist his half-formed inclination to set the King at
liberty, while, on the other hand, he was desirous to
recommend himself to Cromwell and the Parliament,
because he felt persuaded that even if King Charles were
at liberty they would still remain in power, and the King
would have to escape to France. Thus did Colonel
Hammond endeavour to reconcile duties entirely incom-
patible in order to recommend himself to all parties, and,
with his head full of indefinite ideas, he resolved to seek
an interview with Cromwell at Derby House. Being,
however, aware that any personal advantage which might

73

accrue to him depended upon the King's remaining a close prisoner in his power, he increased the strictness of his orders, doubled the sentinels upon their posts, and stopped, as he thought, the only means of communication with the Royalists, by forbidding the attendance of Charles Harcourt upon the King. He had learnt through spies that some plot was on foot among the Royalists to release the King from his captivity, but he was not aware of how far it had gone ; and, feeling sure that all would be safe for a day or so at all events, he left the castle the morning after he sent the letter to Dr. Russell.

Mrs. Wheeler, with Frances disguised as her assistant, under the name of Mary, had, fortunately, presented themselves at the gateway an hour before he started, or they would not have been admitted. As it was, they were subjected to close scrutiny by the sentinels, for the coarse brown frock, and close cap under which she had thrust all her beautiful hair, could not disfigure the refined beauty of Frances' face and form, nor could her courage and presence of mind prevent her from feeling an agony of shame as the soliders stared at her in open-mouthed astonishment.

Mrs. Wheeler, fearing lest they should suspect any-thing, turned round hastily.

" Come along, Mary, my girl," she said ; " you're a'most out of breath coming up that hill, I warrant ; it is uncommon steep, but we cannot waste our time, with all the King's linen to get up afore nightfall."

And so they passed on without further remark. In the laundry they busied themselves about their work, Frances finding in it her best antidote against the mingled fear and wonder which, in spite of her best efforts, the strangeness of her position called forth in her.

Towards noon Firebrace came into the laundry.

"Mrs. Wheeler," he began, in a loud voice, so as to be heard by the sentinel outside, "can you let me have some clean damask for his Majesty's dinner-table to-night?" And then, entering further into the laundry, without waiting for a reply to his first question, he added, in a lower tone: "Saw you aught of young Harcourt when you were in the village yesterday? His Majesty marvels he comes not to the castle to-day."

"The Governor," replied the washerwoman in the same low tone, "has issued orders that no one is to have access to the castle till his return. Yonder," pointing to Frances, "is young Harcourt's sister in disguise as my assistant; she has important papers," and Frances, quick as lightning, produced them; "think you you can take them to the King?"

"They must be concealed," replied Firebrace, "for I am narrowly watched."

At that moment there was a loud rap with a halberd on the door, and a soldier entered, tall and broad-shouldered, with a forbidding cast of countenance.

"How now, Master Firebrace? King Charles will have to wait for his dinner, if you make no better haste than this. Mrs. Wheeler must have some interesting news, to keep you so long in this steaming laundry."

"So please you, sir," said Mrs. Wheeler, "I was but explaining to him that it was through no fault of mine the insignia of his Majesty's damask is so crumpled in the wash"; and here the dexterous woman seized upon a pile of napkins, between the last of which she slipped the papers which she had taken from Frances. "Pray, Master Firebrace, make my humble apologies should the King be angry; it was the fault of that idle slut I have dismissed."

The soldier cast a hasty glance in the direction of Frances, who was busying herself about her work with her back to him, but Mrs. Wheeler, trembling lest his curious eyes should penetrate the disguise, continued :

" Sad times these, Major Rolph ! not a girl could I find willing to come inside the castle, though I hunted through the village. I had to betake myself to Newport before I could get one ; and in one of the small houses there I found this lass, who said she'd be willing enough to come if I would protect her. Protection, a fiddlestick ! I said——"

While the washerwoman was rambling on in this way, Frances placed the pile of clean damask in Firebrace's hands, saying : " Use them from the bottom, please, sir : the top ones are still damp."

And then Firebrace, who understood the hint, left the laundry, followed by the Major, not before the latter had turned to stare once more rudely at Frances.

Master Henry Firebrace had already made good use of the short time he had spent at the castle ; he was of a good-humoured, genial disposition, always willing to assist those who worked with him, and thus he became an universal favourite. He had with great caution sounded the few members of the Royal household, and he had discovered that Osborne, the gentleman-usher, Captain Silas Titus, and Dowcett, the clerk of the kitchen, were loyal to the King ; two of the sentinels, by name Burroughs and Cresset, were also to be trusted ; and he so far gained the confidence of one of the porters, as to be permitted to assume his duty of waiting at the door of the backstairs while the porter was absent at supper. In this way he obtained a series of uninterrupted inter-courses with the King.

Anxious, however, to avoid being discovered, he bored a hole in the wainscot behind the hangings, which was safer than the opening of the door, for, upon the least noise, by letting fall the arras, all was safe. By this means

Firebrace resolved to deliver to the King, that evening, the important despatch which lay concealed in the linen.

The King was in the habit of retiring to his chamber directly after supper ; and Firebrace, having first made himself acquainted with the paper, which was, indeed, addressed to him, took up his station by the door opening upon the backstairs, when the porter had, as usual, taken his departure.

Firebrace listened anxiously for a minute or so,—all was perfectly still within the Royal chamber ; no sound could be heard save the monotonous scratching of a pen, now and then interrupted by a deep sigh, so he gently raised the arras, and giving the peculiar tap, which was the understood signal between Royalists of those days, he slid the paper through. Immediately he heard the King get up from his chair, walk across the room, and presently the paper, one end of which he still retained, was taken by the King, while he said, in a low, clear voice : " Have you any news for me to-night ? "

" I pray your Majesty to read the contents of this paper carefully, and place your answer here to-morrow night, unless you can at once impart to me your pleasure concerning it."

" I will read it forthwith," replied the King ; " meanwhile I will give you my answer to your communication of yesternight, respecting the goodwill of Captain Titus towards me ; and, I pray you, forward it without delay to that gentleman. Have you heard any tidings of young Charles Harcourt ?—he has not come to any harm, I trust."

" So please your Majesty, the Governor has issued orders forbidding any one access to the castle during his absence, and a special order to him."

" How came you by this paper, then ? " said the King.

" The laundress, Mrs. Wheeler," said Firebrace, " returned this morning before the Governor left the castle, and she brought with her a new assistant, who is no other than Charles Harcourt's sister in disguise ; she gave me this paper, concealed among the clean damask."

" What ! the fair maiden who presented me with a rose as I rode through Newport that unlucky day, and asked God's blessing on my hapless head ? May God reward her for her courage and her loyalty ! I fear me it will never be in my power to do so."

The last was said so low that Firebrace could scarcely hear it, and shortly afterwards he heard the King walk back to his table at the other extremity of the room and begin anew to write. There was a pause of a few minutes, which Firebrace employed in reading, by the light of his small lamp, the letter to Captain Titus, which had been delivered open and unfolded into his hands.

It was as follows :*

" CAPT. TITUS,

" Let those officers you told me of know that as my necessity is now greater than ever, so what service shall be done me now, must have the first place in my thoughts when ever I shall be in a condition to requite my friends and pitty my ennemies. I comand you (when you can do it without hazard to yourself or them) that you send me in particular the names of those who you thus finde sensible of their duty and resolved to

* The letters and papers of Capt. Titus were sold, not long ago, to the British Museum. Among them is the series of fifteen letters written by the king from Carisbrook to Captain Titus. These letters are written on pieces of paper of various sizes and shapes : some on the full size of half-a-sheet of foolscap, others on merely scraps of little more than an inch in breadth, and, with the exception of the first, in a feigned hand, having the most important portion in cipher. (See *A Narrative of the Attempted Escapes of Charles I from Carisbrook.* P. XI and p. 107.) Facsimiles of No. I and No. XI of these letters are inserted in this story, Pp. 78, 122.

discharge the parts of true Englishmen. Lastly, assure
every one, that with me, present services wipe out former
falts.   " So I rest
                    " Your assured friend,
                              " CHARLES R."

Shortly after Firebrace had finished the perusal of this
letter, the King again approached the chink and slid a
paper through.
    " Let my loyal friends have this," he said, in the same
undertone of voice ; " I will be ready on the day they
mention, and only too thankful to try any means of
escape from this weary prison ; but, Firebrace, how do
you propose that I should get out of this room ? "
    " Through the window of your bed-chamber, Sire,"
replied his faithful servant ; " if there is room for your
Majesty to pass."
    " I am sure I can easily get through," said the
King.
    " Is your Majesty quite certain it is not too
narrow ? "
    " I have tried with my head," again said the King ;
" and where that can pass the body can follow."*
    " But to put it beyond all doubt, I would propose that,
to make it a little wider, the plate should be cut to which
the casement fastens at the bottom."
    " I tremble lest that should make a discovery," the
King hastily answered ; " if you will prepare all things
else, I am confident that will not impede me."
    " Then," said Firebrace, " your Majesty is disposed
to make your escape on Thursday night next. I will make
everything ready, and toss something against the window
which will be a sign for you to put yourself out, and let

* See *Ashburnham's Narrative*, Vol. II, p. 124.

yourself down by a silk cord, which is, I believe, already in your possession."

" I have it," said the King.

" It is about the time the porter generally returns, so, with your Majesty's permission, I will drop the arras over the chink. May the holy angels watch around you, to succour and defend you from your enemies ! "

" Amen ! " replied the King.

And now the chamber was perfectly still, and the passage where Firebrace was stationed cold and dark. He had replaced the arras, and was standing in the usual place occupied by the porter, when he heard a stealthy footstep creeping down the passage. It did not come from the backstair, the way which the porter always returned, but from the opposite direction ; and, dreading lest he should be discovered, Firebrace hastily extinguished the lamp before the person, whoever he was, could round the corner of the narrow, intricate passage. The footsteps approached nearer and nearer, and presently a hand grasped his shoulder, and the Governor's voice said, in a hissing whisper : " How now, Saunders, sleeping on your post ! "

Firebrace retained sufficient presence of mind not to start at this most unexpected interruption. " I was not sleeping, an' please your Excellency " ; and he tried to assume the gruff tones of the porter.

" Then why is your light out ? " said the Governor. " There is treachery brewing, and I will be at the bottom of it. Has King Charles retired to his chamber ? "

" Faith, your Excellency is more like to know about that than I am," said Firebrace, still in his character of porter.

With a muttered oath Colonel Hammond passed on ; and Firebrace, rejoicing at his narrow escape from discovery, owing to the intense darkness of the passage, hastened to warn the King of approaching danger by a knock, which, in this case, was treble, low, with a distinct pause between each knock.

Directly after, the porter returned, breathless with the speed with which he had run up the stairs. " The Governor has come back," he said, in terror ; " has he been here ? they say he is visiting all the posts, as there is an alarm of the King's being about to escape to-night."

" He came," said Firebrace, " but it was dark, and I counterfeited your voice ; so, if you keep your own counsel, you are safe " ; and Firebrace went in search of Captain Titus, to deliver the King's letter into his hands.

There was a great stir in the castle. Colonel Hammond, by means of the treachery of one Lowe, the postmaster at Newport, had discovered a great part of the plot— fortunately not all—nor could he arrive at any of the names of the people concerned in it. Thinking the escape might be effected that very night in his absence, he returned to Carisbrook, and lost no time in inspecting all the posts in person, as has been already seen. He then made strict inquiries of his chief officer, Major Rolph, if any one had been admitted into the castle since he had left it. No one had come in that day, save the washer-woman and her girl. Colonel Hammond said that he had not seen them, although he had granted them admittance ; and he wished them to be sent at once into his private room. Mrs. Wheeler and Frances felt no small degree of apprehension when they got this order. There was, however, no help for it, and in a few minutes they found themselves in the Governor's presence.

Colonel Hammond was in an ill-humour, having been thwarted in his purpose ; and it was therefore with some sharpness that he said, " What kept you all last night in the village, woman ? " and he fixed his eyes angrily upon Mrs. Wheeler.

" So please your Excellency," she began, in great trepidation, " I was in great straits to find an assistant for the laundry. It's more work than I can do myself, so much clean damask required, it would take more than three people's work to——"

" Pshaw ! " said the Governor, stamping his foot. " You will keep me here all night ; did you find a girl to help you ? "

" Please your Excellency, not one of them durst venture up to the castle, they were so afraid, until at last, when I was nigh worn-out with hunting after them and arguing with them, I betook me to Newport, where I found a nice tidy girl, a thought delicate-looking, but for all that a willing one to work, and——"

" Is that she ? " said the Governor, desirous of putting a stop to such a torrent of words ; " tell her to come forward."

Mrs. Wheeler had had her reasons for running on in this way, wishing to accustom Frances to her situation before she should be called upon to speak. But now the time had come, and Frances, unable to screen herself any longer behind her kind protectress, advanced timidly and made a low curtsey. Whereas before she had been deadly pale, the excitement of the moment caused a deep flush to suffuse her face, making her so lovely, in spite of all the disfiguring effect of her disguise, that Colonel Hammond started up with an exclamation of astonishment.

" Great heavens ! I never saw such a likeness ! " and then, aside, " it is Alice as she was twenty years ago— the very same, there is no mistake—her height, her colouring, her own modest manner."

Colonel Hammond's confusion had given Frances time

to recover herself. A faint inkling of what was passing
in his mind dawned upon her, and she prepared to play
the part of a stupid village girl.

" What is your name ? " at length stammered the
Governor, aware that the soldiers in the room were
exchanging looks of surprise at his demeanour.

" Mary Trattle, an' please your Excellency," drawled
out Frances, so as to disguise her naturally sweet, clear
voice.

" Have you—have you ever been anything else ?   I
mean, have you been long a laundry-maid ? "   •

" Anan, your Excellency," she went on, in the same
tone.

" What are your parents, how old are you, where
do you live ? " said the Governor, all in the same
breath.

To all these questions Frances replied by a look of
feigned stupidity, and Colonel Hammond, thus baffled,
muttered to himself : " Pshaw ! what a fool I am !
She is not really like." With a strong effort he turned
from her, and angrily addressed Mrs. Wheeler. " I forbid
your stirring out of the precincts of the castle on any
pretext whatever, either you or your assistant. There is
treachery at work somewhere."

" As your Excellency pleases," rejoined Mrs. Wheeler,
sulkily.

" You may go now," said the Governor ; " and mark
what I say—woe to any one who dares to disobey my
orders ! "

On the following morning, very early, between three
and four, Firebrace was awakened by a shake from a
heavy sleep into which he had fallen, after having lain
awake half the night busying himself with anxious thoughts
about the King's escape. Rousing himself with a start,
he grasped his pistols with one hand, while with the other

he caught the hand that had seized him. But there was no cause for alarm on his own account, for it was a loyal friend, Captain Titus, who stood by his bed.

"Firebrace," he said, "that villain Hammond dared to disturb the King's rest last night."

"What!" said Firebrace, now wide awake; "how in heaven's name could he get into the King's chamber?"

"By some secret door of which we know not, for I dare be sworn he passed none of us who were sleeping in our usual places outside the Royal bed-chamber, when about an hour ago I was roused by the sound of a scuffle inside the room, and making bold to enter, on account of his Majesty's gracious letter which you delivered to me yesternight, I found the King standing before the fireplace, where some papers were burning, which Hammond attempted to snatch from the flames, but which his Majesty guarded so well that they were nearly all burned. The King looked pale, and his dress disordered, as if slipped on in a hurry, and Hammond's countenance was very black. I asked him what he did in the Royal bed-chamber at that late hour of the night, and threatened to report him to Parliament as having traitorous designs upon the King's life, if he did not at once leave his Majesty in peace. Whereupon he said, half ashamed and half angry, that he was Governor of the castle, and not I, and he would have me mind my own business. To which I replied, ' You may be appointed Governor of the castle, or, if you like the title better, the King's Jailer, but you can have no orders for this unwarrantable conduct, more befitting a thief or an assassin than a gentleman and a soldier.' He could make no answer, except that I should pay for this, and slunk away much ashamed. When he was gone his Majesty told me the villain had come in to search his cabinet for papers, but, owing to your warning of last night, the King had placed them all in the pocket of his clothes, which he hastily slipped on, hearing a noise in his room. The cowardly ruffian carried his insolence so far as to attempt to search the King's pocket, whereupon his Majesty dealt him a box on the ear, and although my tongue almost refuses to speak such sacrilege, the impious wretch struck his Majesty again, and a scuffle ensued. The King, fearing that he would gain possession of the papers by main force, thrust them into the fire, and was defending them when I entered. They are all burned, so nothing has been discovered ; but his most sacred Majesty got a hurt on his face by a knock against the edge of the table."

Firebrace listened with breathless eagerness to this narrative, clenching his fist with fury when he heard of Hammond's violence to the person of the King. " The villain ! the sacrilegious, impious villain ! " he exclaimed, as he ground his teeth with rage ; " but we must get his Majesty safe out of his clutches, otherwise I would proclaim him a villain to all the garrison, and take my chance of being hung for mutiny."

" I pray you do nothing so rash," said Captain Titus ; " patience, we must succeed to-morrow night, and then, when the King is at liberty, we can punish Hammond as he deserves."

" O Titus ! " said Firebrace, " my mind misgives me sorely as to the narrowness of the window. The King is confident he can pass through, but he hath such a broad chest, I fear he will not manage it."

Captain Titus looked grave. " He is not wont to be too sanguine about matters in general," he said ; " I think he must have good reason for what he says ; meanwhile I have a paper for you to deliver to the King's friends, which his Majesty wrote in a hurry, after Hammond left us, urging upon them the imperative necessity of not altering the day fixed for the escape. How will

you manage to convey it, together with the paper you
received from him last night, to the other agents in this
plot ? "

Firebrace reflected for an instant. " I have it," he
said ; " in case we were prevented from leaving the
castle, Colonel Legge is to come disguised as a beggar
with the king's evil, to ask to be touched by his Majesty ;
all such are admitted, and I will manage to give him both
papers as he leaves the castle."

" I commit mine, then, to your charge," said Captain
Titus ; " and I must now go back to my post, or that
wretch will discover that I have been absent."

King Charles kept his chamber the early part of the day,
and did not leave it until the afternoon, when he resorted
to the bowling green for the hours of recreation granted
to him by his jailer. He looked pale and displeased ; an
unusually severe expression had taken the place of his
wonted look of dignified resignation. His face was cold
and proud, his bearing more than usually majestic, and on
one temple was a slight bruise, the palpable evidence of his
nocturnal combat. Colonel Hammond was forced to
attend him in his walk, but he slunk behind like a beaten
hound, and obsequiously tendered his services on every
trivial occasion. His Majesty deigned not to take the
slightest notice of him, whereas on former occasions he
had always conversed with him for courtesy's sake,
though ill enough disposed to do so. To-day the King
addressed all his remarks to his attendants Dowcett and
Firebrace, as if there was no one else present. The
Governor inwardly chafed greatly at this neglect, but
dared not manifest displeasure, knowing how much he
had been to blame in the affair of the preceding night.
Moreover, he was very doubtful how his conduct would
be looked upon by Parliament, to whose ears he made
sure the Royalists would speedily carry the tale of the

night assault, as they pleased to term it, upon the King.* He was frightened also when he perceived the visible mark of his violence on the King's temple, for in spite of his misfortunes, captivity, and a rude treatment at the hands of his subjects, " such a divinity," to use Shakspeare's words, did still " hedge the King," that Colonel Hammond felt himself almost guilty of sacrilege.

At length the hour arrived when it was customary to allow the diseased persons to present themselves before the King and be touched for their distemper, and many flocked in.

The loyal feelings which were still smouldering, despite the distracted state of the times and illgotten success of the Parliament, revived in these poor wretches as they approached to be cured of their horrible disease, and beheld the King.   They fell on their knees before him, they kissed his feet, they implored blessings on his head, a speedy deliverance from his prison, and a glorious return to his throne.

" God bless your Majesty !   May God, who is the King of kings and Lord of lords, bless your Majesty ! and may He send a heavenly guard of angels to replace the earthly soldiers of whom your enemies have robbed you ! "

Such exclamations and prayers could not but be gratifying to the King, whose countenance relaxed from its stern look of displeasure into a melancholy smile. He continued to touch the diseased persons, reverently uncovering his head as he said the appointed form of prayer, and then hanging the gold coin round their necks, which was to complete the cure ;   and sometimes he slipped a broad piece or so into the hands of the very poor. Firebrace was eagerly on the watch for Colonel Legge,

* Mr. Ashburnham published a pamphlet immediately after this event, entitled *The Fatal Blow ; or, the most impious and treasonable fact of Hammond in offering force unto, and hurting His sacred Majesty, discussed.*

and soon recognized him in the garb of an old beggar-woman with a crutch, who hobbled up to the King and kissed his hand with rapturous delight. The disguise was so complete, that even the King did not penetrate it ; and this was perhaps fortunate, as, had he done so, he might not have been able to restrain his joy at seeing again one of those three devoted servants who were so dear to him. Firebrace seized an opportunity, when the Governor's attention was otherwise engaged, to slip the two scraps of paper into Colonel Legge's hand as he approached the entrance to the bowling green, having received which, the gallant gentleman hurried away with strides hardly befitting the character he had assumed.

When all had been touched, his Majesty withdrew to his chamber. The occupation in which he had been engaged had soothed his ruffled spirits. It served to recall to him that at least that afternoon he had been a King, exercising an attribute belonging only to kings, and which would remain his, however much his enemies might wrest from him his royal insignia of his office, and deprive him of the power belonging to it.

The gratitude and prayers of the people had touched his tender and compassionate nature, which, while it stimulated him to kind and benevolent actions, restrained him, alas ! too often to his own personal harm, from ever doing a hard-hearted thing.

It was, then, in a calmer frame of mind that the un-fortunate sovereign retired to rest that night. He felt no fears that the Governor would again disturb him, for, with his quick perception of character, he saw that Colonel Hammond was ashamed of what he had already done.

On the other hand, the King rejoiced in calling to mind the faithful friends who watched around him, and in reflecting on his probable deliverance from captivity on the ensuing night, while a yearning almost unendurable seized him to know if indeed the labours and efforts of so many devoted friends would at last be crowned with success.

How often, at certain periods of our lives, do we wish with passionate eagerness that God would allow us to lift for an instant the veil of futurity ; and how often do we bless Him again and again, because that which in our blindness we asked for was not granted to us !

CHAPTER VI

" The wall is high ; and yet will I leap down :
Good ground, be pitiful, and hurt me not ! "

King John, Act IV, Sc. 3.

ONE other circumstance strengthened the determination
of the Royalists to carry their scheme into effect. It was
in the afternoon of the 20th, the very day which
they had chosen, that Frances had gone to the great
kitchen at the castle in search of some boiling water.
Mrs. Wheeler, although anxious to spare her as much as
possible any real labour, was obliged now and then to
give her some work to do for fear of arousing the suspicions
of the garrison. Frances was looking forward with delight
to returning home, having accomplished, at some cost to
herself, the dearest object of her heart. She found by
experience that the disagreeable and dangerous nature
of her undertaking had not been overrated by her
mother, and she was glad that her self-imposed task was
nearly finished. With the sanguine nature of youth, she
would not allow herself to imagine that the attempt of
that night, which they have contrived with so much toil
and pain, would be otherwise than successful. She was
returning to the laundry, her mind occupied with pleasant
thoughts of her mother's joy at receiving her back, when
her attention was arrested by seeing Major Rolph enter
the kitchen. His duty in no wise called him there, and
there was something in his countenance which made her
think he had come there for no good purpose. She resolved therefore to remain where she was, concealed by

one corner of the dresser. The King's dinner was about to be served; the cook had left the kitchen in search of some necessary article or other, and the Royal pages had not yet come to fetch the repast. Now was Major Rolph's moment; he advanced with stealthy steps towards the tureen of soup which was smoking on the table, and, taking from his pocket a small packet, opened it and shook in the whole contents. He then peered in to see if anything would betray him. No; the powder had immediately dissolved, and a few bubbles here and there on the top only showed that it had done its work. Not content with this, Major Rolph uncorked the King's bottle of sack, and poured the contents of a similar packet into it, then corked it again, and hastily withdrew, his face deadly pale, with a gleam of triumph in his eye, not having observed Frances, who remained horror-struck at what she had witnessed. No sooner was he gone than she advanced, and, without a moment's hesitation, threw the whole of the soup out of window on to the grass outside; she then poured the poisoned wine after it, and finally smashed the bottle to pieces lest it should be employed again. The noise of its breakage brought the cook back in a fury. Perceiving the broken bottle and empty tureen, she flew upon Frances, and there is no saying to what lengths she would have proceeded in her passion had not the King's pages, Firebrace and Dowcett, appeared.

"Sir! please, sir!" said Frances, flying to Firebrace for protection, "they were poisoned, the soup and the wine, so I have thrown both away."

"Poisoned!" said Firebrace; "the villains! The Parliament shall hear of this; and you," turning to the cook, "are like to lose your place and your head together."

The cook was too much astonished to find words to defend herself, but Frances interposed:

" Sir, she had nothing to do with it ; she had left the kitchen. It was put in in her absence by——"

" Whom ? " said Firebrace.

" Major Rolph," said Frances, in a low tone. " Do not betray me—he will kill me."

" The villain ! the cowardly assassin ! the scoundrel ! " said Firebrace ; and then, after a moment's reflection, he added, " We will say nothing of this to-night to the Governor or to the King. His Majesty has already enough to disturb him, without this treachery to add to it. The Governor I will inform myself to-morrow ; so, cook, give us what else you have prepared for the Royal supper-table, and I will procure another bottle of wine. We will invent some tale of this having been thrown down and smashed, which indeed it seems to be."

Whatever gossip may have taken place respecting the attempted poisoning of the King, nothing reached the Governor's ears, and the Royalists studiously concealed it from their master, thinking it might unnerve him for the great enterprise of that night.

The King supped without taking any notice of the smallness of his repast, his thoughts were so fully occupied, and retired early to his chamber. The extreme darkness of the night favoured the undertaking. Firebrace first ascertained that all were at their posts—Worsley and Osborne outside the counterscarp with the horses, and Burroughs and Cresset, the two faithful sentinels, on guard. Then between twelve and one he stationed himself outside the Salisbury Tower, where the King was confined, and gave the sign agreed upon.

His Majesty put himself forward, but, alas for that unhappy fate which seemed to attend him in every crisis of his life ! now, when it was too late, he found himself mistaken. The passage, as Firebrace had only too truly surmised, was too narrow, and the King stuck fast between the bars of the window, not able to get forwards or backwards !

The agony of his faithful servant below when he heard the King groan with pain can easily be imagined, and how ardently he longed to assist him. Almost distracted with grief, he clambered up on to the ledge of wall upon which the King was to have alighted, by means of the rope, had he been able to pass through his window, but further Firebrace could not get ; the rugged walls of the tower rose sheer above his head, and he dared not call to the King for fear of arousing the garrison. At last, to his inexpressible relief, the King's light was set in his window, a sign that he had extricated himself from his painful position, and also that all was at an end for that night.

Now it became an urgent necessity to communicate to those who were waiting outside the failure of the attempt, and this Firebrace could find no better way of doing than by throwing down stones from the high wall where he had clambered up, and whence he was to have let the King down. Fortunately, this proved so effectual that they went off, and no discovery was made.

It is a popular belief that on this occasion King Charles remained between the bars of the window till released in the morning, but this is untrue. Contemporary accounts give an altogether different version of the affair. Mr. Ashburnham, to whom the whole account was of course at once communicated, as he was to have furthered the escape when the King landed in Hampshire, writes in his narrative :

" Hee got back again without anie certaine notice taken by anie man but by him (Firebrace) who waited to have served him when he had come downe."*

Although the proposed escape had been so artfully

* Ashburnham's *Narrative and Vindication*, Vol. II, p. 124.

contrived as to have been kept an entire secret from the Governor, Cromwell's spies, who were dispersed all over the Isle of Wight, somehow discovered it, and communicated it to Cromwell, who at once sent intimation of what had been attempted to Colonel Hammond, giving the names of all those who were concerned in it, and the night the attempt was to have taken place. On the receipt of this letter the Governor was greatly enraged to find how nearly his prey had slipped through his fingers, and he began to feel he could trust nobody. He sent for Firebrace, and by threats and bribes tried to extract from him some account of the transaction, but Firebrace contrived to baffle him, as did others whom he also tried to examine.

Meanwhile, the chink not having been discovered, the correspondence continued as before, and on the very night succeeding the 20th, King Charles slipped a paper through it to say : " The narrowness of the window was the only impediment of my escape, and therefore some instrument must be had to remove that bar, which, I believe, is not so hard to get, for I have seen many, and so portable that a man might put them into his pocket : I think it is called the endless screw, or the great force. . . . I command you heartily and particularly to thank in my name, A. (Cresset), C. (Colonel Legge), F. (Dowcett), Z. (Mr. Worsley), and him who staied for me beyond the works (Mr. Newland), for their hearty and industrious efforts in this my service ; the which I shall always remember, being likewise confident that they will not fail in so good a work."*

When Firebrace acquainted the King of the stir that the arrival of the letters from Derby House had created in the castle, and how the Governor was bent upon

* See *A Narrative of the Attempted Escapes of Charles I from Carisbrook Castle*, by George Hillier, p. 113.

finding out if those whose names were mentioned in the letter had indeed connived at the attempt of March 20th, the King implored him not to imperil his life by remaining in the castle, lest it should be discovered how large a share he had had in the scheme. His Majesty even said he had letters of importance to be conveyed to the Prince, his son, which he would intrust to no one but Firebrace, in order thus to induce him to leave the castle. But Firebrace begged to stay till he was absolutely dismissed by the Governor, as he could not bear to leave his Royal master in such distress. For this, however, he had not long to wait, for a few days later Colonel Hammond sent for him again and told him that, having received further intelligence about him, he must now dismiss him from attending upon the King. In four days from that time he must leave the castle. This was partly designed as a trap, but Firebrace behaved with so much prudence and discretion that he was able to settle such a way of correspondence that his Majesty should not want constant intelligence from his friends, even supposing that Charles Harcourt was not allowed to resume his duties as secretary. Firebrace had, however, shrewdly imagined, and communicated his surmise to the King, that, as no possible suspicion could attach to Charles in this last attempt to forward the escape, he would probably be allowed to return to the castle to take the place of those who were dismissed on account of their share in it, and thus another escape attended with better success might easily be devised.

It was fortunate the Royal captive had this prospect to look forward to, as his spirits sank very low when, for a second time, all his friends were removed from him. About three weeks after Firebrace's dismissal, Captain Titus, Burroughs, and Cresset were sent from the castle by order of the Governor, under the authority he had received from the Derby House Committee, wherein he was empowered " to place and displace such persons as were to attend the King, as he should see occasion."

At the same time also it was suggested to Colonel Hammond by Major Rolph that the laundress and her assistant were not to be trusted either. Major Rolph had never discovered why his poison had not taken effect upon the King, and concluded that either the soup had not been tasted, neither the wine drunk, or else that he had been duped by the person who sold him the powder as poison : because the cook, the only other person acquainted with what had really become of it, save Firebrace, Dowcett, and Frances, had been bribed to secrecy, lest, by revealing how the poison had been discovered, Frances might have been suspected and sent away from the castle, or perhaps even met with a worse fate at the hands of Major Rolph, who was an unscrupulous villain. Firebrace had also seized the opportunity, when the cook was horror-struck at the intended poisoning of the King, to work upon her feelings, and make her solemnly swear, that not only would she never assist at any project of this nature herself, but also that she would never be absent from the kitchen during the preparation or serving up of the King's repast until she had placed it in the hands of the Royal pages, or Dowcett, who was clerk of the kitchen, that nothing of this kind might ever occur again.

Nevertheless, although Major Rolph knew nothing of all this, he had discovered by eavesdropping and prying about the laundry that the washerwoman and her assistant were friendly to the King, if not agents in the plans for his escape. He lost no time in reporting this to the Governor, who sent for them and told them that they also were dismissed from serving the King.

When Frances once more stood before Colonel Ham-

mond, the likeness to her mother again appeared to him
so striking that he could scarcely contain himself. Had
the slightest suspicion of the probability of her being a
disguised daughter of Madam Harcourt's occurred to
him, had he even known that that lady had a daughter,
all must have been discovered. But he was actually
ignorant of the fact, for although he had been present
at Newport when Frances had presented the rose to the
King, he never found out that she was the sister of Charles
Harcourt, not noticing him among the crowd of people.
Just as Mrs. Wheeler and Frances, rejoicing at her two-
fold escape, were curtseying themselves out of his presence,
the idea flashed across his mind that she was the girl who
had presented the rose on that memorable day.

" Ha ! " he said, starting from his reverie, and turning
suddenly to Frances ; " were not you the maiden who
presented King Charles with a rose as he rode through
Newport ? I thought I had seen your face before, and
now I recollect."

A thrill of horror ran through Frances, her knees
trembled, she became deadly pale, and she thought all
was lost. Mrs. Wheeler came to her assistance in a
timely manner.

" Why, stupid, have you lost your tongue ? There
is nothing to be afraid of. His Excellency will bear you
no ill will for that, I warrant. Of course she was, an'
please your Excellency ; and the rose came out of her
father's garden, old David Trattle, as lives by the market-
place, a stout old cavalier soldier, craving your Excellency's pardon, who lost his arm at Naseby, so please
your Excellency."

" Umph," said the Colonel ; " I see now why you were
so willing to bring her up to the castle—I wish I had
known of her parentage first, that's all. But you leave
the castle this moment," he added, striking the table

G

with his fist to give emphasis to his words, " and you will
not come back here, either of you, with my good-will,
unless you wish to know the look of the inside of one of
the dungeons yonder. Take them away," he said, addressing the soldiers, " and see them off the premises, and
down the hill into the village, and then leave them."

Mrs. Wheeler's ready wit had just saved them, and
Frances, when at last they were rid of the troublesome
company of the soldiers, expressed her gratitude in the
warmest terms.

" If it had not been for you," she said, " I was lost,
for I did not recollect that he was ignorant of the name of
the girl who gave the King the flower, and I could not
deny that I had done so."

" Poor dear, poor little lamb," said the kind woman,
soothingly, " thou hast borne thyself bravely ; and it
is through no fault of thine his Majesty is not now at
liberty, and able to reward thee for thy courage. But
we must try again : we will never leave him where he is
so long as we have any of us a breath left in our bodies ;
and here we are at thy mother's house, and main glad
she'll be to see thee, I warrant."

It is not necessary to picture the rapturous delight
with which Madam Harcourt received her child, returned
safe out of so many perils, or the joy of her brothers and
grandfather. In truth, they had begun to be alarmed
as her stay at the castle prolonged itself indefinitely, and
to fear that it would be long before she would be able to
leave it.

Frances had much to tell, and it was with horror that
the faithful loyalists listened to the account of the intended poisoning of their master. Of this they knew
nothing, because Firebrace, when dismissed, had set off
at once for Netley Castle to tell Mr. Ashburnham what
had occurred, and to procure the forcing-screw for his

KING CHARLES I AND BISHOP JUXON, PRINCE HENRY, PRINCESS ELIZABETH.
AFTER BLACKBURN.

facing p. 98.

Majesty. He had only stopped one moment as he passed Madam Harcourt's house to say Mistress Frances was well, and he thought young Master Harcourt would soon be allowed to go up to the castle and see her himself. They already knew of the failure of the scheme for the King's escape, and the cause of it, through the other agents, John Newland, Edward Worsley, and Colonel Legge.

Mrs. Wheeler was amply rewarded for her invaluable protection of Frances. Gladly would Madam Harcourt have fed and lodged her in her own house for some time to come, but she feared if this was known it would excite suspicion ; so, with her purse well filled, despite her indignant refusal of all money, that good woman departed for Newport to visit her friend, old David Trattle, who did not exist only in her imagination. From thence she professed herself willing to assist any scheme that might be set on foot for delivering the King.

The likeness of the supposed washerwoman's assistant to Madam Harcourt in her youth had brought that lady vividly before Colonel Hammond's mind, and he began to reflect that the steps which he had lately taken were not at all likely to find favour in her eyes. He turned over in his mind how he might recover himself in her good opinion, and, at the same time, do his duty, as he termed it, as Governor of Carisbrook, or rather jailer to the King. He had almost forgotten Charles Harcourt in the exciting events which had lately occurred, and he remembered that he, at all events, had never been in the least implicated in the plot. The King was very low and out of spirits now all his friends were gone.

"What will become of me," thought the selfish Governor, "if he were to destroy himself or die of melancholy ! He seems fond of that boy, and he is but a stripling—no harm could possibly arise out of allowing

him to come and write notes from those crabbed old
books. It's a mercy they keep my Royal prisoner (I wish
it had pleased Heaven to make him any one else's charge !)
so well employed. Besides, I owe him something to make
up for that scuffle a few weeks back, in which I was to
blame."

With these thoughts in his mind, Colonel Hammond
resolved to go down to the village and pay a visit to
Madam Harcourt, hoping thereby to combine two things,
namely, to see Alice Harcourt and to give her son leave
to return to the castle.

Leaving word that he was only going for an hour to
the village, and begging Major Rolph to keep a strict
watch upon the sentries, he sallied forth on foot. It was
hardly half a mile's walk to Dr. Russell's lodging, where
he thought he would go first, and persuade that gentleman
to escort him to his daughter's house ; there Colonel
Hammond durst not go alone, fearing he might be refused
admittance. When he reached the lodging he was informed that the person he inquired for was out, up
yonder at Madam Harcourt's. He slipped a broad piece
into the woman's hand, and bade her go there and say
that a gentleman—the Governor, in fact, of the island—
would be obliged to Dr. Russell to favour him with five
minutes' interview at his lodging.

Scarcely an hour had elapsed since the return of Frances
from the castle when the woman arrived at Madam
Harcourt's house with the message for Dr. Russell from
the Governor. They were all terrified, thinking that he
must have infallibly discovered who the washerwoman's
girl really was. Their first care was to conceal Frances ;
and then Dr. Russell, determined to put a bold face upon
the matter, accompanied the woman who had brought
the message back to his lodging.

He found the Governor in his private room, walking

up and down. One glance at his face, and the good
clergyman was satisfied that no discovery of the kind
they dreaded had been made, for the Colonel's face wore
the anxious expression of a man about to ask a favour,
and not of an angry man who had been deceived.

"In what way can I serve you?" said Dr. Russell,
gravely.

"Dr. Russell, I know what you think of me," said the
Governor, impetuously; "lying stories are afloat about
me—indeed, I but do my duty, if you only knew how
hard that was."

"Colonel Hammond, there is an old French proverb,
Qui s'excuse s'accuse. I have not accused you of anything; if your own conscience does, and you are come
to me for spiritual advice, that is another matter."

The Governor turned impatiently away, muttering
something about "Papistry"; but then, recovering
himself, he said:

"Dr. Russell, the long and the short of the matter is
this: I have again been obliged to dismiss all the King's
attendants on account of their treacherously conniving
at his escape." Dr. Russell could scarcely restrain a
disdainful curl of the lip at this speech. "The King is
low and unhappy; your grandson is a harmless youth,
and is free from all blame in the matter I spoke of. I
notice his presence seems to cheer the King, and the
object of my visit this morning is to give your grandson
leave to serve him again as secretary."

He looked keenly at Dr. Russell as he said this, hoping
to discover something from his face, but this remained
calm and impassive, though inwardly the good doctor
was overjoyed.

"My grandson," he said, "will be very glad to tender
his poor services to his Majesty. I will not disguise from
you that he finds great delight in serving a master who

was and still is, regardless of all that has come and gone, beloved by all."

Colonel Hammond shrugged his shoulders.

" Yes, I find that to my cost, as far as his personal attendants are concerned. But if your grandson keep from treachery, and be open and above board, I care not if he attend upon the King for a couple or so of hours every day."

" So be it, then," said Dr. Russell.

But Colonel Hammond had only as yet accomplished half his object, and now he said, abruptly :

" Dr. Russell, in order to pleasure you and your family, I have done what is scarcely consistent with my duty ; will you, in return, grant me the favour of an interview with your daughter Alice—I mean Madam Harcourt— in order that I may place the pass which is to give her son admittance to the castle in her own fair hands ? "

" That must be for her to decide," said Dr. Russell, a shade of displeasure clouding his brow ; " but if you will return with me to her house I will give your message to her, provided always that you faithfully promise to abide by her answer, and retire without delay should she refuse to see you."

" On my honour, I promise," said Colonel Hammond, and they both set off together for Madam Harcourt's house.

Leaving the Governor in the porch, Dr. Russell went at once into the parlour where Madam Harcourt was sitting, talking over with her sons what Frances had related to them of her stay at the castle. Of course, the account of Colonel Hammond's insolence to the King on that memorable night had not been omitted in the relation, and had filled them with indignation. Arthur was storming against the Governor's cowardice and villainy, while Charles sat by white with compressed fury, longing with all his soul to punish the insult as it deserved, when Dr. Russell entered.

" Hush ! " he said, sternly, to Arthur, " or your foolish violence will ruin us all—he is here in the porch."

" Who ? the King ? " cried Arthur.

" No," said Dr. Russell, " Colonel Hammond." He signed to Charles and Arthur to leave them alone, and then, turning to his daughter, " Alice," he said, quickly, " with regard to Frances, all is safe, nothing has been discovered, and Colonel Hammond only came to give Charles leave to resume his attendance upon the King ; he wants to see you and tell you so himself, and give the passport into your hands. He is now waiting in the porch."

" I cannot see him, father," said Madam Harcourt.

" O Alice, I fear me everything will be lost if you do not ; Charles will not be allowed to go to the castle, and then how shall we help his Majesty ? "

" I cannot help it, father," she continued, in a still fainter tone of voice. " I cannot do evil that good may come ; it would be wrong ; he would construe it into encouragement, if I were to allow him to see me, whereas I feel an aversion amounting to loathing at the mere sound of his name, especially after what I have just heard. Do not urge me, father, I cannot do it. I do not fear about Charles, and even if it were so, we could find some other way of helping the King. Please go at once and tell him to begone—I can never see him."

Very reluctantly did Dr. Russell convey the unwelcome message : " My daughter cannot see you," he said to the Governor. " I am sorry you have put yourself to the trouble of coming here."

. " Will to-morrow suit her better ? I will come to-morrow, or the next day—any day."

"She will never see you," said Dr. Russell, in as firm a tone as he could command.

A dark scowl came over Colonel Hammond's countenance. "Good evening, Dr. Russell," he said, lifting his hat haughtily; "your obedient, humble servant. In that case I cannot give the passport to your grandson."

"As you please, sir," replied Dr. Russell, with equal coldness; "it is yours to give or to withhold."

Colonel Hammond walked away; but he had not gone above a few steps when, turning hastily, he held out to Dr. Russell the piece of paper, which, in his anger, he had crushed up small in his hand. "Take it," he said; "give it to the boy: I will protect him; and tell your daughter not to think so hardly of me. I am not the villain she takes me for." And without waiting for thanks, or looking back, he strode away.

Dr. Russell turned again into the house, with the scrap of paper, which was so invaluable to them, in his hand. He held it up triumphantly. "See, Alice, I have got the passport!"

"But is he gone?" said Madam Harcourt; "and does he understand he is never to come here again?"

"I delivered your message, word for word, and I think there can be no mistake as to the meaning of it. At first he went away in a great passion; but then, all of a sudden, he turned and held out this paper, bidding me tell you he would take care of the boy, as he called Charles; and that he himself is not so great a villain as you imagine him to be."

"He does not know, then," said Madam Harcourt, without the slightest sign of relenting in her face, "that I am acquainted with his late vile assault upon the King. Father," she added, in a softer voice, more like her usual gentle self, "you see now I was right in refusing to see him. Had this passport been given me as a reward for granting him an interview, I never could have suffered it to be employed, as I should have received it on false pretences, and hereafter Colonel Hammond would have just cause to complain of me, if I had refused anything he might have asked me. As it is, this passport is a free gift to my son, without conditions ; we may, therefore, make what use of it we please with a clear conscience."

" You were right, Alice," said Dr. Russell ; " in my anxiety to clutch at any straw whereby we might save the King, I lost sight of other duties. But now let us call Charles ; he will be overjoyed to hear that he may again return to the castle."

CHAPTER VII

" Let our halls and towers decay,
    Be our name and line forgot,
Lands and manors pass away,—
    We but share our monarch's lot.
If no more our annals show
    Battles won and banners taken,
Still in death, defeat, and woe,
    Ours be loyalty unshaken !

" Constant still in danger's hour,
    Princes owned our fathers' aid,
Lands and honours, wealth and power,
    Well their loyalty repaid.
Perish wealth, and power, and pride !
    Mortal boons by mortals given ;
But let constancy abide,
    Constancy's the gift of heaven."
                    Rokeby, Canto V, s. xxiv.

IT had been a severe blow to Charles Harcourt, when he was told that he was forcibly cut off from serving the King ; for since the monarch's arrival at Carisbrook the whole aspect of the lad's life was changed. Hitherto he had fulfilled the routine of his home duties with conscientious perseverance, making his mother his first care, cherishing her with all the warmth of filial love, and striving to fill the dreary void which he felt the loss of his father must leave in her heart. As he grew from boyhood into youth, ambitious dreams would sometimes fill his mind of following his father's footsteps, and dying, if need be, in the same noble cause. But the war was for the present suspended, and he knew there was nothing to be done, except patiently to bide his time, and wait till he saw his way more clearly towards joining the

Royal army. What could he effect by himself, in his early youth, barely eighteen, with a brother, enthusiastic and courageous certainly, but two years younger than himself, and only one follower left out of the retainers his father had taken with him to battle ? He must at least be content to remain quiet till the scattered Royalists had reunited themselves, and had organised some distinct plan of action.

But since the event of last November all was different, and duties of a nature above and beyond anything he had dared to picture to himself, even in his wildest dreams had fallen to his lot. The abstract feelings of loyalty, which he shared in common with every generous heart, had received a more definite and practical character from his personal intercourse with the King, and he had become devotedly attached to his Royal master.

Although in his general conduct Charles Harcourt appeared so grave and quiet, seldom giving way to those bursts of enthusiasm in which it was Arthur's delight to indulge, his feelings were none the less deep ; and his whole spirit revolted against the oppressive nature of the King's confinement. Had the King been at liberty, at the head of his troops, on the winning side, with everything falling out prosperously for him, it is probable that Charles, although willing enough to serve him, would not have felt the same devotion to his cause, the same burning enthusiasm, the same passionate longing to lay down his life for him, as now when, unfortunate, abandoned, and in daily peril of death, either by open trial and condemnation, or by secret attempts to assassinate him, the King spent day after day in the dreary monotony of a prison life.

From childhood upwards Charles Harcourt had always been irresistibly drawn towards the unfortunate. He had never found any pleasure in fighting with the winning

side ; and a triumph over the vanquished, however much
the fallen foe had deserved his fate, was alien to his
nature. To lead a forlorn hope, at whatever peril to
himself, or, if this could not be, to comfort the sorrowful,
and try by any sacrifice to restore what had been lost,—
these were his real delights ; and when thus engaged,
his fine face would glow with generous satisfaction and
his eyes beam with affectionate gladness. The bare idea
of oppression was hateful to him ; and that it should be
exercised towards his King, for whom he felt what might
now be called a superstitious reverence, made him shudder
with indignation. To apply the language which Burke
used a century later, when speaking of an equally unfortunate sovereign, Charles thought " that ten thousand
swords would have leapt from their scabbards to avenge
even a look that threatened him with insult." The feelings
of the Royalists of that day for their King would be called
overstrained and exaggerated in these hard-reasoning,
unenthusiastic times. Great faults had those gallant
Cavaliers, but, nevertheless, cheerfully sacrificing all
that this world holds most dear, they followed their
master through every stage of his ill-fated career ; they
fought for him again and again, in battlefields, where the
odds against them were ten to one ; when beaten out
of the field they shared his wanderings ; when imprisoned
they strove, at any risk to themselves, to set him free ;
in a word, they devoted their whole lives to his service,
and very often ended them by a gallant death in the same
loved cause. Such virtues may be easily scoffed at, but
not so easily imitated.

When young Charles was informed by his grandfather
that Colonel Hammond had again given him permission
to serve the King, his joy knew no bounds. He ran to
impart the good news to Arthur, who was in the garden
with John Newland. All were equally glad, since by this

restored access to his Majesty they hoped soon to set on foot another plan for his release—John Newland and Arthur had been deeply grieved at the failure of the last attempt. All their measures had been taken with great care, and they had engaged the best sailing vessel in the island, which would have taken the King over to Hampshire in a surprisingly short time. However, they bribed the fisherman to keep the boat in readiness, should they again require it, agreeing to give him three days' notice. Nothing could now be settled till the return of Firebrace with the forcing-screw and orders from Netley Castle.

Newland had taken a very early opportunity of expressing to Frances, who, on the departure of the Governor, had emerged from her hiding-place and joined them in the garden, his warm approbation of her courageous conduct. They had been friends from their earliest youth, so a great intimacy had grown up between them.

" You do not mind my telling you how noble I think it was of you, my dear Frances, do you ? " said John, tenderly. " I have been wretched while you have been away. I could not bear the idea of your going to the castle ; but now it is all over, and you have come back, I must tell you how I admire your courage and loyalty."

" I do not mind your telling me so," said Frances, " if you think so. I do not deserve that you should speak of me in that manner ; but I care for your approbation as much as if you were my own brother," and she looked affectionately at Charles.

" But," said John, impatiently, " I do not want you to think of it quite in that way."

" I cannot help what you want," said Frances, with a merry laugh, and she ran back towards the house.

" Frances," said John, not wishing to be thus baffled, " I have something very particular to say."

" I don't believe it," said Frances.

" It is about the King."

" Well ? "

" Do tell me how he looks."

" Alas ! I never saw him," said Frances, with a little sigh ; " but I think he knew I was there," and she disappeared into the house.

" John," said Charles, seriously, " I shall be going to the King to-morrow ; can I take any message from you to him ? "

" No," said John, resuming his gardening, " unless you like to say that I would willingly take ten times the trouble and run ten times the amount of risk to serve him. I feel very envious of you, Charles. I do so long to look upon his Majesty's face again."

On the next day Charles Harcourt resumed his attendance upon the King.

Colonel Hammond, who had subsequently felt secret misgivings as to the prudence of his conduct in admitting Charles again into the castle, determined to keep a strict watch upon him when there. He escorted him into the Royal apartment, and prepared to remain there some time. In his presence both the King and Charles were obliged to place a strong restraint upon themselves, so their meeting was very quiet. The King merely observed, when young Harcourt knelt to kiss his hand, " We are right glad to see you again " ; and Charles could scarcely prevent his eyes filling with tears, when he saw how sad and altered his master looked. Many silver threads were beginning to show themselves among his long curling locks, immortalised in the well-known picture of him by Vandyke ; his countenance was melancholy and dejected, and his dress not arranged with his usual scrupulous care. All these signs Charles Harcourt, who was a keen observer, took notice of, and they made his heart sink. He could not bear to see, although he could scarcely wonder at it, how much the monotony of his captivity was preying upon the King's spirits. He also noticed a marked coldness in his manner to the Governor, who appeared to be so much galled by it that, unable to conceal his mortification, he left the room. Then the old freedom of intercourse between the King and his secretary was renewed.

"Charles," said his Majesty, "nought but evil luck hath attended me since I saw you last. I am sick at heart; all my friends are gone; and I am ready to despair of ever regaining my liberty. This dungeon is only the first step to the scaffold."

"Say not so, my dear master, for God's sake say not so; it breaks my heart to hear you speak after this fashion. It shall not be. We will never cease trying till we have rescued you. I feel confident the next attempt will be successful. Say not all your friends are gone; they are close at hand, though expelled from the castle. Master Firebrace we expect back to-night with news from Netley Castle, and, we trust, with the screw for your Majesty to remove the bar."

"Alas!" said the King, "talk not of *the* bar; there may be twenty to remove in the next apartment which I occupy, for my jailer Hammond, fearing lest my escape should be too easily contrived from my present residence, on account of my friends being so intimately acquainted with it, purposes to remove me to another part of the castle; and I learn that before I am conveyed thither another bar is to be placed between the stone mullions, and a platform is to be thrown up beneath the window, where a sentinel will be stationed to shoot me down, I presume, if I attempt to escape through it."

Charles Harcourt scarce knew what answer to make. The tone of dejection in which the King spoke distressed him sorely, and he racked his brain to find some comfort to administer to him.

After a short pause, the King said :

" I had well-nigh forgotten, being so eaten up by my own troubles, but in good time I recollect—tell me of your sister. I trust she reached her home in safety, and that no evil befell her for her noble effort on my behalf. It was bravely done."

" She will be overjoyed to hear of your Majesty's kind inquiries concerning her," replied Charles. " She returned quite safely, undiscovered, and is now at home with my mother."

And then, hoping to divert the King, he told him of her last interview with the Governor, and of the timely assistance rendered by Mrs. Wheeler.

" Stay," said the King, in a graver tone of voice ; " but she hath suffered, I fear me, great annoyance for my sake. If ever I am restored to my throne I will not forget it ; and as that is unhappily still far to seek, I pray you take her back this as a testimony of my regard, and bid her not to measure the extent of my gratitude for her noble deed by this paltry trinket."

As he spoke he took a ring from his finger, which he handed to his secretary.

Charles was inexpressibly touched.

" Sire," he said, " I cannot find words to thank you sufficiently on my sister's account for this gift, so largely enhanced by your gracious words of approbation. It will be an heirloom in our house for ever."

There is no pleasure to be compared with that of making others happy ; and the consolation which the King derived from so deeply gratifying his faithful young secretary went some way towards restoring to him the calm equanimity which was natural to him.

He was able to discourse more hopefully concerning a new project for escape ; and he gave a letter into Charles's keeping for Captain Titus, telling him why he had not

yet changed his lodgings, and desiring advice as to the
removal of any obstruction in the way of their plan,
which he might find in his new apartment. It was written
in cipher, and signed " J.", the letter chosen by the King.
Charles Harcourt had barely time to hide this paper,
which was written on a very small scrap for the better
concealment of it, in his hat betwixt the felt and the
lining, when Colonel Hammond returned, and announced,
without any pretence of ceremony, that " the time was
up ; he must go." Then, suddenly recollecting himself,
on observing Charles's look of astonishment, he added,
" that is, if his Majesty require your services no further."

The King's lip curled with inexpressible scorn.

" We thank you for your courtesy, for all it came
rather late," he said, with bitter irony, to the Governor,
and held out his hand to Charles, who kissed it. " You
may retire," said the King ; and young Harcourt withdrew from his presence with as much ceremony as if his
Majesty had been in his own palace at Whitehall. Colonel
Hammond felt compelled to do the same, to his infinite
disgust ; but he made up for it when outside, by grasping
Charles tightly by the arm, and never relaxing his hold
till they were outside the castle gateway, when he almost
pushed him down the hill.

Firebrace did not arrive that night ; but on the following morning early Mrs. Wheeler appeared at Madam
Harcourt's house with a letter, which had been placed
in her hands late on the preceding day by one of the
Royalist agents from Netley Castle, as they were not able
to trust the post-office.

It was addressed to Charles Harcourt, and was from
Firebrace himself, to the effect that he was now in hiding,
and could not leave London. He had been recognised,
and his movements were closely watched ; but he had
managed to see Mrs. Whorwood, a lady well known to the

H

King, and he had consulted her as to the best way of procuring the screw which was required. She had first enlisted the services of the celebrated astrologer, William Lilly, and by his advice she had employed one George Farmer, an ingenious locksmith in Bow Lane, to make a saw to cut in sunder the iron bars, as well as furnish a sufficient quantity of aqua-fortis for the same purpose. With these articles, a man in whom Mrs. Whorwood placed confidence had been despatched to Portsmouth, whence he was to proceed to Newport by fishing-boat. Firebrace then suggested that Arthur should employ the fisherman, whose services they had engaged, to convey him to Portsmouth, where he could meet the messenger, and bring back the instrument and bottle of aqua-fortis to his brother, who must find some means of conveying them to the King.

Firebrace was still ignorant as to whether Charles had been allowed to return to the castle ; but he urged upon him the necessity of finding some other means if this was not permitted. " Osborne and Dowcett are not dismissed from the castle," he added, " although they are removed from attending upon the King : through their means the articles might be conveyed to him." In conclusion, the letter said : " Lose no time, for every moment his Majesty's life is in danger. I have it on good authority that the army perpetually send messages to Colonel Hammond to destroy him, and Major Rolph is a double-dyed villain." The letter was dated the 24th of April ; it was now the 28th. No time must therefore be lost ; and Arthur, acting upon Firebrace's advice, went at once in search of the fisherman who had promised to serve them. By means of a bribe he persuaded him to convey him at once to Portsmouth, where, after waiting some time, they observed a man approaching the wharf, answering to the description of the messenger given by

Firebrace, for he was " a fat plain man." Arthur, who was waiting on the wharf, advanced towards him, and said, in a low voice :

" In the King's name ? "

To which the man replied readily :

" God save him ! " and pointed to the basket over his shoulder. It had the appearance of a fish-basket, and contained about half a dozen fine mackerel, which the messenger had procured at Portsmouth that morning.

" You seem to have had good sport," said Arthur ; " better than we have, for not a fish have we caught this day. I would gladly buy your ware. Will it please you to step into my boat, that I may show your mackerel to my friend, who is a better judge of fish than I am ? "

" Assuredly," replied the man.

As soon as they were in the boat they carefully raised the mackerel, and concealed among the straw at the bottom lay the instrument and bottle of aqua-fortis.

Arthur hastily scratched a note to Firebrace :—

" Received safely, and shall be forthwith conveyed to ' J.'   " ARTHUR HARCOURT."

" Is the King in good health ? " said the man, in a low tone of voice.

" But indifferent, I fear," replied Arthur. " My brother sees him daily. Tell Master Firebrace this."

Then the fisherman put off, and, the wind being favourable, they made a good passage to Newport, where Arthur, taking leave of the fisherman, flung the basket over the shoulder, and set off briskly home. He met with no obstacles, and so far all was well ; but the most difficult part was yet to come. How should Charles convey his precious charge past the scrutinising glances of the sentinels, perhaps even of the Governor himself ? Frances declared her willingness to undertake the task.

Regardless of the Governor's threat of a dungeon, she would disguise herself as a fisherman's daughter, and take the basket containing the fish, with the instruments, to the cook, and get her to convey them to his Majesty in a dish. But this plan, though ingenious, was scarcely feasible, as the Governor was always present when the King dined or supped. Nevertheless, part of it was adopted, for it was settled that Charles should take the mackerel himself to the cook, and while she was examining them, take out the screw and bottle of aqua-fortis, and conceal them somewhere about his person. After his admittance into the castle, he would not be liable to be searched again on his way from the kitchen to the Royal apartment. They could hit upon no better plan, so Charles resolved to play his part boldly on this occasion, and carry this scheme into execution. He marched up to the gateway with the mackerel still in the basket, and the instrument wrapped round in withs of straw, so as to make a kind of false bottom to the basket, in case the sentinels, in prosecuting their strict search, should remove the fish. He had to submit every time to being searched, otherwise the Governor would not have allowed him to enter the castle. On this day the soldiers asked him many questions concerning the mackerel. " Where he had caught them ? " " What was he going to do with them ? " " Whom were they for ? "

" For the King," said Charles, firmly ; " and I will take them to the kitchen myself, if you will show me the way."

" You may find it yourself," they replied ; " we have something else to do besides running after boys with fish."

Charles would have found this no easy matter, had not good fortune thrown Dowcett in his way while he was vainly hunting among the passages. No one was by, so

Charles made him understand as quickly as he could what he wanted to do, and Dowcett showed him the way to the kitchen. They durst not remove the instrument in the passage lest they should be discovered.

Once in the kitchen, the difficulty was comparatively over, for while the cook was busily engaged in examining the fish, Charles fumbled in the straw under pretence of searching the basket for more, and thus extracted the forcing-instrument and bottle of aqua-fortis, which he concealed in his clothes. Dowcett then showed him the way to the King's new apartment, for the change in his lodging had taken place. Fortune had so far favoured them that Colonel Hammond was for once out of the way, and Charles was able not only to give the King the instruments whereby he was to effect his escape, but also to conceal them in his chamber. Young Harcourt had besides a bundle of letters to deliver to his Majesty, which had been placed in his hands at the same time as his own letter from Firebrace.

There was one letter from Captain Titus which appeared to trouble the King, as it was evident some treachery was at work, and this was again to be traced to the master of the post-office. The King had long since ceased to communicate with his friends in England by the post, always trusting his letters to faithful messengers ; but as for his foreign correspondence with the Queen and the Prince, his son, he had of course been compelled to trust these to the post, written in a feigned hand and super-scribed to a friend at Paris, whence they were forwarded to the Queen. Now it was plain from Captain Titus's letter that this had been discovered and reported to the committee at Derby House. Captain Titus implored the King to trust nothing further to the post, and then submitted the second scheme for escape to his Majesty for his approval.

When, by means of the forcing-instrument, the King had succeeded in removing the bar, and had emerged from his chamber, which was about ten feet above ground, he was to proceed across the bowling-green to the counter-scarp of the castle, whence he was to descend and be received on the other side by Mr. Worsley and Mr. Osborne, as under the former arrangement. Mr. Newland was again to be in waiting with the boat—this reached, they were to cross at once to Hampshire. Horses would there await them, with relays to convey the King to the residence of Sir Edward Alford, near Arundel. From Arundel he was again to journey on horseback to Queen-borough, in Suffolk, where a ship was prepared to trans-port him to Holland, as the most favourable place of safety.

This was the scheme ; and it appeared very good in all its points to the imprisoned monarch, but, having once failed in the part which he had himself to play, he felt now as despairing about his success as he had formerly been confident. His new lodging was in the house of the chief officer, Major Rolph, a man who was in every way odious to him ; not only was Rolph forbidding in appear-ance, but also coarse in manner, and with a loud, harsh voice. He made no secret of his personal dislike to the King, and of his entire want of sympathy with his mis-fortunes. Ralph was originally a shoemaker, and he was now a major in the Parliamentarian army. His was one of those low, bullying natures which take delight in trampling on the fallen, and he found a special pleasure in annoying the King as far as he dared. He was a shrewd man, and, partly by resorting to the lowest arts of eavesdropping, partly by cunning, he had discovered that a second scheme for the King's escape was on foot : and as Colonel Hammond had failed to find any proofs which he could fasten upon the accomplices in the former

attempt, Major Rolph now proposed to him not to throw
any hindrances in the way of the Royalist plans, but, on
the contrary, to let them mature themselves, that so
they might be able to apprehend in the very act all who
took part in them. By means of spies, intercepting letters,
and other arts, they must find out when it was to take
place, so that their prey might not slip through their
fingers. Major Rolph was busily engaged in proposing
this plan to the Governor when Charles Harcourt arrived
at the castle. They did not know he was the.e till Colonel
Hammond, who went to apprise the King that he was
ready to attend him should he feel disposed to take any
recreation, found Charles in the Royal apartment employed as usual in copying

Hammond started when he saw who it was, and other
thoughts different from those he had just been consider-
ing flashed through his mind. What and if he should
deceive Major Rolph also, and really forward the escape
for the purpose of setting the King free ! How grateful
would the Royalists be to him then ! how differently
would Charles Harcourt think of him ! Perhaps he would
influence his mother in his favour, and then what a
reward would be his ! But on the other hand he might lose
his life, and certainly his position and interest, for betray-
ing trust ; and, hastily dismissing the first dream, he
accosted Charles, bowing slightly to the King, as he felt
constrained to do whenever young Harcourt was
present.

" How long have you been here ? " he said,
roughly.

" About two hours," replied Charles, rising from his
seat ; " the sentries will tell you they let me pass after
the usual examination."

" You may retire now," said the King, " I do not
require your services any more to-day."

At dinner-time, that same evening, King Charles observed with pleasure that Osborne had resumed his place of gentleman-usher, and stood at his right hand holding the King's glove, the office which it had formerly been his duty to discharge. Moreover, after dinner, when his Majesty sought to put on his glove, he felt a little obstruction in one of the fingers, and on examining it, in the privacy of his chamber, he found it to contain a billet with words to this effect :—

" SIRE,

" I am, as before, bent on forwarding any scheme for your release, therefore I know not why the Governor has restored me to my post of gentleman-usher. Let your Majesty beware especially of Major Rolph. He is a scoundrel. I fear treachery surrounds you, but I pray you believe me, till death,

" Your Majesty's devoted servant,

" OSBORNE."

The King was much comforted to find Osborne still faithful to him ; he needed not the warning to beware of Major Rolph, for already he shunned him as an enemy. If possible, this prime confidant of Cromwell's had rendered the King's captivity still more unendurable, constantly intruding upon his privacy on the slightest pretext, stationing himself at the presence-chamber door, and refusing to show any mark of respect when in the Royal presence. No wonder that he was odious to the King, whose spirits were so much affected by this additional vexation, that he could scarce keep up any heart at all for the new enterprise. Meanwhile the preparations went on at a brisk rate, for his friends—who were indefatigable —sought to cheer his Majesty with constant correspondence, which was faithfully transmitted to him by Charles.

Firebrace, at imminent personal risk, had returned to the Isle of Wight. In his anxiety that no way should be left untried, this devoted servant hit upon yet another scheme. He learned through Osborne that the porter of the back stairs, whose goodwill he had himself gained when at the castle, and whose business it was to carry up coals for the King's chamber after dinner and supper, had expressed his willingness to change clothes with the King. He further proposed to remain in the Royal apartment while his Majesty made his escape as porter. Now Firebrace, wishing to have more than one string to his bow, by means of young Harcourt acquainted the King with the porter's offer. His Majesty did not think " this new way," as he terms it in one of his letters " was to be rejected," adding that he would abide by Firebrace's decision, " although the easie or difficult removing of the barr will cast the scales in my judgment betwixt the two wayse."*

It was now the beginning of the month of May, and the plans of the Royalists were fast approaching to maturity ; indeed, any further delay would have been most inexpedient, as much depended upon the darkness of the night.

Firebrace being again compelled to leave the island, Captain Titus came to Southampton to take his place, and the King's correspondence with him was carried on with uninterrupted regularity.

Mr. Worsley, who had remained concealed at Gatcombe, in the disguise of a servant, went often to visit Captain Titus, that they might arrange their plans, and very frequently he was the bearer of the King's letters, which

* Letter No. V.—See *A Narrative of the Attempted Escapes of Charles I from Carisbrook*, p. 145.

he received from Charles Harcourt.* One of these, bearing date Sunday, May 14, was as follows :—†

" W.

" Yesterday I receaved fower letters from you with a great number of others from divers of my friends, as one from my wife and from Lady Carlisle, as many from Mrs. Whorword : the lyke nomber from both Cresset and Lowe, besydes a great bundle from D. Fraizer and Col. Legge, also fower from Firebrace and one from T. This I give you an account of, because not having tyme now to write to any of thease my friends, I desyre you make my excuse to them, and lett them know that I have receaved all theire letters : now as to your Answer : all that I have to say to yours of the first of this month, is, that as I see that you are well satisfied with me, so I am with you (for those two of the 12th, that wch is out of cypher I know not what you meane by it) ; but I thanke you for the Advice you give me in the other, though I finde that our design as to this place must be altered. Now as to that of the 9th my answer is, that for my landing-place you must appoint it ; likewise you and Worsley must tell me where I shall take boate. I can write no more concerning my escape until I have consulted with Osborne : in the mean tyme I must tell you that now I can asseure you that no letter of myne hath miscarried, for I have had an Answer of that from my wife, wch I suspected, there being no other in possibilitie of doeing harm. Before this morning I could not

---

* These letters from the King to Captain Titus are fifteen in number. They are authenticated as genuine, and are mostly in cipher. Two of them, No I and No. XI (the one which it is known Mr. Worsley did actually convey to Captain Titus), are inserted as specimens of the correspondence.—See *A Narrative of the Attempted Escapes of Charles I from Carisbrook*, p. 153.

† All the proper names, and all the details connected with the escape are written in cipher.

speak with Osborne, wch hath given me tyme to write thease two inclosed ; that superscribed in French is to my wife, the other to Mrs. Whorwood. This last I thought fitt to write to encourage and thanke her, because I fynde that she hath assisted you in providing the ship. Now as for our great business. I desire you to begin to waite for me on Monday next and so after, every night for a weeke together, because one night may faill and accomplish it, and being both troublesome and dangerous to send off word to you ; and for the time here, you must know that it is my chamber window on which I must descend, the other being so wached that it cannot be cut, wherefor I must first go to bed so that my time of coming from my chamber may be about eleven at night : for the rest you with Worsley must compute how soone I can be with you. This is as much as for the present I can say concerning my escape, and I hope such as will give you reasonable good satisfaction : but I desyre you to send me speedie word if anything that I have written be obscure, or not full to what you desyre to know ; also where I shall take boate and where lande, likewise you must give me a passe word that I may know my friends in the darke. And now I have no more to say, but what I cannot say according to my mynde, wch is to express my satisfaction and thankes to you, for what you have done for me in this Business ; only this, you shall fynde me really,

" Your most asseured constant friend,

" J."

" You must remember to leave horses so that I have no stay between my landing and Queenborough."

This letter was perused by Captain Titus with great anxiety. It certainly was not in a very hopeful strain, and in former letters to him the King had expressed great doubts as to whether he should find it possible to remove the bar of his window. The instrument which had been already supplied was a kind of coarse file, and his Majesty feared that he would scarcely have time, between the hour of his retiring to bed and the hour appointed for the escape, to saw through the bar. He also thought that the noise might attract attention, and being since the failure of his last attempt most distrustful of his own judgment, he communicated all his doubts to his faithful servants. Captain Titus wrote him a reassuring answer, suggesting aqua-fortis as a means of overcoming the difficulty the King had mentioned, and finally, he arranged with Worsley that, should his Majesty approve, everything should be made ready for Wednesday, the 24th of May. However, on hearing subsequently from the King that the course of the guards was altered, and that the turn of the two faithful sentinels did not come till the Sunday following (the 28th), the escape was finally arranged to take place on that night.

Meanwhile Charles Harcourt was allowed to continue unmolested his attendance upon the King, and his visits were the only break in the weary captivity of the lonely monarch. The King had become deeply attached to his young secretary, and would often call him " his namesake," as the intimacy brought about by the peculiar circumstances of the case, between the generous youth and the captive monarch, increased and strengthened every day. The faithful lad tried, by every means in his power, to cheer the King ; he would tell him of the indefatigable efforts of his friends, of their devoted love and self-sacrifice, counting all as nought if they could but set him free, and how daily every morning and evening prayers were offered up for him by Dr. Russell, in Madam Harcourt's house, where many of the villagers would often resort, to mingle their tears and supplications with him for the speedy deliverance of their sovereign. The public feeling also was beginning to show itself more favourable to the Royal cause. In Wales the Royal standard was unfurled : in Kent, men flocked to the trumpet of Goring ; while in Essex the last gallant effort was made in the memorable siege of Colchester. The Cavaliers were known to be in every county in England, but alas, they were at too great a distance to communicate with each other, and so could not hit upon any united plan of action. In the Isle of Wight, compassion for his strict captivity, and a general discontent with the existing government, had made the inhabitants desire fervently the release of their lawful sovereign. Had not Colonel Hammond sent for perpetual reinforcements, so as to make the whole island one vast garrison, the islanders would have risen, and, overpowering the mere garrison attached to the castle, have delivered the King from his confinement.

However, the time fixed upon for the escape was now rapidly approaching, and the Royalists were confidently looking forward to the end of their master's irksome imprisonment. Nevertheless, Charles Harcourt could not help entertaining some misgivings. He felt there was something suspicious in their being suffered unmolested to mature all their schemes ; the absence of any obstacle in their way suggested to his mind the idea of the King's enemies being acquainted with their project, and purposely refraining from interfering with it, that they might be the better able to apprehend those who were engaged in it, or else do some grave mischief to his Majesty. He resolved to keep a careful watch ; and his suspicions chiefly fastened themselves upon Major Rolph, who, he felt sure, would be restrained by no feelings of honour or generosity from resorting to the foulest deed of violence, to hinder them at the last from

accomplishing their purpose. Of the Governor himself,
during the last fortnight, Charles had seen little or
nothing ; and, far from obtruding his presence upon the
King when engaged with his secretary, in the way he had
hitherto done, he seemed to wish to avoid entirely the
sight of young Harcourt. Moreover, his Majesty informed Charles that when Colonel Hammond did attend
upon him, to perform any necessary function of his office,
his manner had been more deferential ; there was not
so much of petty tyranny in his regulations ; and altogether the King had suffered less annoyance than he had
done since the dismissal of his gentlemen in the early part
of his residence at Carisbrook.

With Osborne the King was often able to interchange
a few words ; and his gentleman-usher, who shared in a
small degree young Harcourt's anxiety, warned his
Majesty concerning Major Rolph, and related to him
some part of the Major's loud and violent conversation
which he had overheard. How Rolph " wished the King
were out of the world, for they should never make any
settlement while he were alive ; that he was sure the
army wished him dead ; and that Hammond had received
many letters from the army to take him away, by poison
or any other way ; but he saw it would never be done in
that place." Once the villain went so far as to make a
confidant of Osborne, and to ask him to join with him,
that they might get the King from thence, and so the
work be easily done. All this Osborne told the King ; but,
notwithstanding, his Majesty bid him keep on familiar
terms with Major Rolph, hoping to make us of his
treacherous scheme in accomplishing his own purpose.

But Charles Harcourt was sad and uneasy when this
dark plot was communicated to him ; he entertained no
hopes of their deriving any benefit from it ; on the
contrary, he feared it would mar all. Connecting what

he heard with the Governor's studious avoidance of him, he feared that Colonel Hammond was privy to the chief officer's scheme, and would allow him to accomplish it all, even to the last deed of villainy.

Still the King was in no wise cast down : any risk seemed preferable to a continuance of his odious captivity, and he bade Charles not to be uneasy about the success of their own plan. Young Harcourt, knowing how much depended upon the King himself in the accomplishment of the escape, strove to assume a cheerfulness which he was far from feeling. He would spend hours at the castle, now he was no longer subjected to the annoying supervision of the Governor, and when they had discussed every possible circumstance connected with the escape, he would read aloud to the King out of his small collection of books. Of this the greater part was Divinity, Bishop Andrewes' Sermons, Dr. Hammond's Works, *Villalpandus upon Ezekiel*, Laud's *Paraphrase upon King David's Psalms*, Herbert's *Divine Poems*, &c. Besides, the King was intimately acquainted with Greek, Latin, French, Spanish, and Italian, which three last he spoke perfectly, and greatly delighted in reading Tasso's *Jerusalem Delivered*, and Ariosto.

At this time the King is said to have employed himself in writing the book entitled *Icon Basilike*,* and the poem called *Majesty in Misery*, which must for ever remain as a faithful and touching picture of his sufferings, together with the patience and fortitude which enabled him so nobly to endure them.

On Saturday, the 27th of May, before Charles took leave of the King, it was agreed between them that the

---

* " Many have not scrupled to ascribe to that book (the *Icon*) the subsequent restoration of the Royal family. . . . The *Icon* passed through fifty editions in a twelvemonth. It was published a few days after the King's execution."—See Hume's *Hist. of England*, Vol. VII, pp. 159, 160.

next day, the Sunday, fixed upon for the great enterprise, Charles should not appear at the castle till late in the afternoon, and then remain with the King concealed in his chamber, in order that he might be at hand to help him to sever the bar, to adjust the cords by which he was to descend from his window, and to protect him against treachery. Colonel Hammond had of late paid so little regard to Charles' visits, that it was thought he might well be concealed without any questions being asked as to whether he had returned home. The rest of the arrangements were all complete. The three soldiers who had been proved faithful were to be on duty at the time appointed. Dowcett was to guide the King to the horses, which were ready provided, and laid at a convenient place within musket-shot of the works, with Osborne and Edward Worsley in attendance. These gentlemen would conduct the King to a creek where lay a boat in readiness, with John Newland and Arthur Harcourt, to transport his Majesty to the mainland, whence he was to proceed as has been already said.

It was with no common feelings of emotion that Charles bade adieu to the King for the last time, as he hoped, in captivity ; but he controlled himself, for fear of agitating his Royal master, and said, in as cheerful a voice as he could assume, " Heaven grant that when I next leave this castle your Majesty may also say farewell for ever to its gloomy walls ! "

" Amen ! " replied the King ; " although, if it be so, think not that I will ever forget the faithful services which have been tendered me during my sojourn here."

CHAPTER VIII

" He died the beautiful death,
  My own brave boy ;
And—break, though it may, in its desolate ruth——
Thy mother's heart, for thy loyal truth,
  Hath passionate joy !
Dead though thou art in thy strength and youth,
  My glorious boy ! "
             Song of a Cavalier's Mother, by J. B. Stone.

THE members of Madam Harcourt's little household had
worked themselves into a feverish state of excitement as
the crisis at length drew near. Now their hopes and now
their fears preponderated, and Dr. Russell found it a hard
task to preserve in them any of that coolness and presence
of mind which he knew would be essential to secure the
success of their great enterprise. Always calm and trustful
he was able to sustain them when, sick with disappointment and baffled by numberless difficulties, they were
almost ready to despair. Again, on the other hand, when
their hopes of success were too high, the good clergyman
would remind them that it might please God to deliver
the King in some other way which they could not understand, and which would seem hard to them : that, after
the example of a Master whom their sovereign had all his
life taken as his pattern, and served as the King of kings,
he might be fitted, through suffering, to inherit an everlasting kingdom, in place of the earthly one of which he
had been deprived.

For, in reality, Dr. Russell shared largely in the misgivings of his grandson. Still, he thought nothing would

be gained by deferring the attempt, more especially as the King's own wishes were so decided as to its taking place at the time agreed upon, but he trembled lest, at the last, when it was too late to go back, they should be betrayed. Madam Harcourt was more confident. She could not believe that Colonel Hammond would be so lost to all feelings of honour as to suffer a villain like Major Rolph to attempt any personal violence against his Majesty.

John Newland, also, being of a buoyant and sanguine disposition, felt no fears on this point. By degrees he and Edward Worsley had procured everything that was necessary for the escape, so far as their share in it was concerned. Knowing of what vital consequence it was to provide a good horse for the King, they had not ceased their efforts till they had secured a beautiful thorough-bred animal, such as his Majesty loved to ride in days of yore. This, with two other swift horses for Mr. Osborne and Worsley himself, had been for the last fortnight in the stables at Gatcombe, carefully groomed and fed by the young master of the house in his temporary disguise as stableman.

It was now some weeks since John Newland had been a disguised inmate of Madam Harcourt's house, and thus neither time nor opportunities had been lacking to enable him to renew his former intimacy with Frances Harcourt. As children they had always liked each other ; he had taken part in all the childish pursuits of Madam Harcourt's family, and Frances had thus learnt to look upon him in the light of another brother. Feelings of a different nature had, however, been gradually awakened in his heart by her innocent, unsuspecting affection, and the confidence which she reposed in him. Since his return from the war and his residence in her mother's house, these feelings had been strengthened by daily intercourse

with her, and the bonds of one great common interest.
They had now assumed a very definite form of love,
while he was seized with a passionate yearning to know
if they had awakened any similar feelings in her heart.
He was five-and-twenty, and the life of hardship and
danger which he had led from his early youth had tended
to develop his character and give him experience beyond
his years. During the early part of his sojourn at Carisbrook he had been impatient of the delay occasioned by
the failure of the King's first attempt to escape, and the
time of waiting had seemed to him very long while preparations for a second attempt were being made, more
especially as Frances was still away at the castle, toiling,
as his fond imagination depicted her, and in danger.
He had never liked the idea of her going there, and, as
time passed on, his anxiety became so intolerable that he
could not bear to stay without being able to see her or
assist her. He had therefore absented himself for some
days on pretence of seeing his friend Worsley. Fortunately for him, he had by chance come back the very
evening of her return, and since then all had been changed
for him. He now made good use of his leisure time in
really doing the work belonging to the character which
he had assumed, and Madam Harcourt's garden had
never been so well tended.

Young Newland found great satisfaction in this joint
labour of love and loyalty, and these two ideas, in-
separably linked together, were perpetually at work in
his brain. Supposing the King made a successful escape
this time, and reached Holland in safety, he knew a long
period must elapse before the Royalists could muster a
sufficient army to support their cause with any success.
Meanwhile he would be at liberty to protect Madam
Harcourt and Frances, if only he had a right to do so.
Otherwise, after their great object had been accomplished,

there would be no reason for his remaining any longer in her house. But, once the accepted lover of Frances, or, as he fondly hoped, her husband, he would be able to assist them, supposing fresh difficulties should overtake them, and to place his comparatively ample means at their disposal. When he thought of this he could scarcely refrain from laying it all at the feet of Frances ; but then, when he reflected on her extreme youth and ignorance of life, he hesitated whether he had a right to claim her affections. " At all events," he said to himself at last, " I will wait till the King is in safety, and then I will see what Madam Harcourt says to it." But this prudent decision was destined to be immediately disturbed by the approach of Frances, who came up to him with bright eyes and eager looks.

" Charles has just returned from the castle," she said ; " the King is quite determined to make the venture to-morrow night." Then she told him of the arrange-ment which Charles had made with his Majesty as to staying to help him to descend from the window. " And O John ! " she added, anxiously (they had always been as brother and sister together), " do you think it will prosper ? Are the horses quite ready and very swift, and is that fisherman to be trusted ? "

As she spoke, and as he gazed at her, so lovely in her enthusiasm, John felt his prudent resolutions fast ebbing away, and her final appeal to his judgment was more than he could withstand.

" Frances," he said, in a tone and manner different to the usual playful one which he generally assumed in his intercourse with her, " with God's help, all will, I trust, be well ; there shall be no effort wanted on our part to secure success, I need scarcely assure you. I will presently go to Gatcombe to tell Worsley what time he is to bring the horses to the counterscarp of the castle, and then I must finally arrange about the boat. But before I go I have something I want to say to you very much."

For a moment Frances looked up at him, wondering at his grave, earnest manner, and then all of a sudden a faint idea of what he was about to say dawned upon her mind.

" What is it ? " she said, in a very low voice, fastening her eyes on the ground.

Without further preface, John began earnestly to plead his cause, telling her how he had always loved her ever since they had been children together ; and that when he had seen how brave and unselfish she could be, he felt utterly unworthy of her ; yet still——and here he took her hand, and his tones became still more impassioned.

" But, John," said Frances, softly, " how can you think of such a thing, with the King in danger, and this awful risk hanging over all our heads ? "

" O Frances ! " cried John, perceiving his advantage, " if the King is freed, if the Roundheads are put to the rout, will you consent then ? "

" I must think ; I cannot say now," said Frances.

" But you are not angry with me ? " said John.

" Angry ! " said Frances. " Why should I be angry ? I wish I could say half what I feel. It makes me proud to think that one so good and brave, whom I have always esteemed so highly, should care for me."

John seized her hand and kissed it before she could stop him.

" You must not," said Frances ; " you must not do so. To-morrow I will tell you." And she turned and went back into the house in a very different frame of mind to that in which she had left it.

Young Newland, who had succeeded, to a certain degree, better than he had dared to hope, went to his friend Worsley at Gatcombe with the King's message.

" Where is John ? " said Arthur, when he saw Frances.
" He need not trouble himself to go to the fisherman, for
I have managed it all."

" He is gone to Gatcombe. I suppose he will be back
presently," said Frances, as quietly as she could.

" That's right," said Arthur. " Oh ! if to-morrow
were but here ! "

Sunday came at last. In the morning Dr. Russell held
a solemn service in an inner chamber of his daughter's
house ; special prayers were offered up for the safe
deliverance of his Majesty from captivity, and the twenty-
first Psalm was selected as a proper psalm for the occasion.
As the little company of faithful Royalists listened to those
words of hope and trust, they forgot their doubts and
fears, forgot the imminent danger before them, their
sorrows and their privations, and only remembered that
amid all the changes and chances of this mortal life there
was One ever ready to help and defend them.

Early in the afternoon John Newland and Arthur had
repaired to Newport, to be sure of the fisherman and his
boat. Captain Titus was to join them there. But before
he went John begged Madam Harcourt to grant him an
interview, in which he urged his suit with all the passionate
fervour of his nature. Madam Harcourt did not lend an
unwilling ear to his proposals. She was quite aware how
much there was to admire and esteem in his character ;
still she was very decided in her opinion that this marriage
must not be thought of for some years. Frances was very
young, and the times were very unsettled. She had come
to this conclusion after a long conversation with her
daughter the evening before, when, in a state of mingled
joy and bewilderment, she had fled to her mother for
comfort and advice. However, Madam Harcourt yielded
to John's earnest entreaties that he might see Frances
and hear her answer from her own lips. It was thus far

favourable to him that her final consent was not to depend upon the success of that night's enterprise. Only, so long as the Royal cause was to be fought for—so long as the King was to be delivered—Frances would allow no other duty to occupy her lover's thoughts, knowing by her mother's sad experience how much such partings must harass the soldier's mind, especially in these troubled times, when the wife must perforce remain in a position of difficulty and peril.

Besides, Frances would not leave her mother. "Charles and Arthur will both go with the King if he is released," she said. "They must do so now : it is their duty, and mother would not hold them back ; but I could not leave her. Perhaps some day you will be able to stay at home, when these terrible troubles are over, and then we will think about it."

With this John was forced to be content, as the best and wisest scheme, more especially as he felt persuaded that it was not any want of love for him which made Frances propose this delay.

Towards four o'clock that afternoon Charles made ready to go up to the castle for the last time. He carried, concealed in his pocket, now he was no longer subject to such strict supervision, another file to complete the work of severing the bar, in case the one possessed by his Majesty should have been broken. Before going, he meant to take leave of his mother and sister, because he intended accompanying the King as far as Queenborough to see him safely embarked in the ship which was to convey him out of the reach of his enemies ; then Charles was to return home till the Royalist plans were definitely arranged. So now, with a courageous, cheerful countenance, he bade his mother and sister farewell. He kissed Frances, and then his mother, with warm affection.

" Mother," he said, " please God I will be true to our motto, if I die for it."

" God bless you, my son ! " said Madam Harcourt, in a faltering voice, for his speech, when he unconsciously repeated his father's words, brought back to her vividly the time when she had parted from her husband never to see him again. " You have been a good son to me and a loyal servant to your King. May God bless you in this your enterprise to-night, and for evermore ! "

She could not speak further, and Charles thought best to cut short the painful scene ; so he kissed her once more fervently, then tore himself away, and went to his grandfather's lodging, wishing to see him alone for a few minutes. He told Dr. Russell what he had kept from his mother, how he meant to go through the window that night first, before the King, so that if there were any treacherous design to shoot his Majesty from below, he might receive the shot instead.

" Major Rolph is capable of anything," he said ; " and he will probably attempt that ; but against it we cannot provide, as we do not even know if he is acquainted with our scheme, and certainly not where he means to conceal himself if unhappily this should be so. In this case he will shoot at the first figure which emerges from the Royal chamber, making certain that it is the King, as he will not know of any one else being there. Should this happen—should the shot prove fatal, give my mother this with my love, and tell her I knew she would not wish it otherwise."

He cut a lock from his hair, and pressed it, with his watch, which had been his father's, into Dr. Russell's hands. Not being able to trust himself further, he did not wait for a reply, but rushed out of the room, and soon found himself making his way up to the castle.

It was a lovely afternoon in May, the air was fragrant

with blossoms, the long grass waved on the castle steep
with tall daisies, whose pure white petals and golden
centres were ever turning towards the sun ; in the hedges
the sweet wild honeysuckle was just beginning to show
itself in long pink and white buds, and briony, with its
curling tendrils, preparing to weave itself into cool green
bowers as the summer advanced.   The birds sang gaily,
the cuckoo went on with its unceasing call, and the
swallows swept round the castle in rapid flights, now
flashing their white breasts and now their purple backs
in the sun, now skimming along close to the ground, now
soaring high, dipping, and turning and tumbling in the
air, the very personification of liberty.

   " Would his Majesty were as free as they are," thought
Charles, as he followed them wistfully with his eyes,
" instead of being confined in this gloomy castle, with its
frowning towers and narrow, cramped area ! "   Then his
thoughts reverted to the enterprise which was to free the
Royal captive from his prison, and to the part which he
would himself have to play in order to accomplish this.
Again the same foreboding filled his mind which the
service of the morning had dispelled.   Charles was no
coward ; and the idea of laying down his life to save the
King filled him with enthusiasm.   All his loyal feelings,
not to speak of his deep personal affection for his sovereign,
tended to make him court, rather than shun, so glorious
an end to his short young life.

   But then he thought of his mother.   " It will break
her heart," was his inward reflection ; " for she loves me
far more than I deserve, dear mother ! " and here a few
natural tears came to his eyes.   " I pray God she may
not grieve for me too much.   She knows it is what my
father would have wished had he been alive.   Arthur and
Frances will still be left to her, and John, who will take
my place as a son."

At last he thought of himself, of the bullet-shot, of the physical pang unknown, which must attend the separation of soul and body, and a cold shudder crept over him ; of his unfitness for death, for he was very humble-minded, and, blameless as his life had been, he felt how much he had left undone, how much more he might have done in God's service. "But God is very good," he reflected ; " and for our dear Lord's sake He will forgive me." And then he thought of the life everlasting, the life of the world to come, where there shall be no more wickedness to grieve over, no more sadness, no more shortcomings, where sorrow and mourning flee away, and God will wipe away tears from off all faces ; and it seemed as if he heard a voice saying, above the song of the birds, above the summer hum of the insects, amid the wind murmuring among the trees, and sweeping the tall grass : " Be thou faithful unto death, and I will give thee a crown of life."

" Even so, Lord Jesus," he said, and bent his head in silent prayer.

These reflections, long as they have taken to relate, passed in rapid succession through his mind, and when Charles recovered his self-command and his usual grave, quiet manner, he found himself in front of the tower-gate.

Everything seemed to favour their scheme, for the sentinels who were to be on guard outside King Charles's window that night were now on duty at the gateway. Their time was nearly up, but they recognised Charles, and let him pass without any challenge.

" Do not let the Governor know I am here," said Charles, in a low voice, and he passed swiftly on to the King's apartments without seeing any one else except Dowcett, who was stationed at the door of the presence-chamber.

Major Rolph, who had before held this post with annoying pertinacity, for the last few days had resigned

it to Dowcett, which to Charles again revealed a suspicious
knowledge of their proceedings. However, the enterprise
must be carried through bravely now ; it was too late
to suggest any alteration, and Charles, whose outward
demeanour did not bear any trace of his recent mental
agitation, was shown into the Royal presence. The King
received him with much joy, and listened with keen
interest when Charles told him of the solemn prayers
which Dr. Russell had offered up that morning on his
behalf. His Majesty sighed when young Harcourt made
an end of his narration.

" I would I had been with you," he said, " for the sour
Presbyterian doctrine, forced upon me by the chaplain
here, goes sorely against the grain. I am often at a loss
to determine whether is greater, the ignorance or the
arrogance of these members of the Solemn League and
Covenant. Several have been here with the pious design
of converting me—or rather perverting me—to their
views since my captivity. Mr. Sedgwick presented me
with a book which he had written, entitled, *Leaves of the
Tree of Life.* I read but a small portion of it, for *me-
thought the author stood in need of sleep.** Mr. Harrison
likewise wished to engage me in a discussion upon con-
troversial points ; but as his logic and his reasoning
power seemed equally at fault, I declined to continue the
argument. I pray you read something to me out of my
small library, to pass the time and work us into a befitting frame of mind for the approaching crisis."

Charles Harcourt took down from the shelf Laud's
Paraphrase on the Psalms, but the King, perceiving it,
said, hurriedly :

" Nay, not that to-day. I cannot bear to think of
that cruel murder of my faithful servant." And his face
wore a troubled look which Charles had never noticed

* Historical.

there before. He hastened to replace the book, and
selected instead one of Herbert's poems. Turning to
" Affliction," one of the King's favourites, and much
marked with his own hand, the last two verses appeared
to young Harcourt to fit in singularly well with their
present condition :

> " O help, my God ! let not their plot
> Kill them and me,
> And also Thee,
> Who art my life : dissolve the knot,
> As the sun scatters by his light
> All the rebellions of the night.

> " Then shall those powers, which work for grief,
> Enter Thy pay,
> And day by day
> Labour Thy praise and my relief,
> With care and courage building me,
> Till I reach heaven, and, much more, Thee."

Thus did the time pass till close upon his Majesty's
dinner-hour, when Charles thought prudent to retire to
his place of concealment, which had been before agreed
upon, between the arras and the wall in the Royal bed-
chamber. A few minutes after his departure the Governor
appeared to announce that his Majesty's dinner was
served.

The King observed Colonel Hammond narrowly, and
marked his restless, frightened manner. His Majesty
was himself in good spirits, and conversed more than
usual during dinner with his attendants respecting the
general state of the kingdom, even addressing now and
then a word to the Governor, who stood by in manifest
perplexity and uneasiness of mind.

Meanwhile, Charles Harcourt had not been neglected
in his concealment, for Dowcett had supplied him with

food from the King's own table ; but he could not touch it in his anxiety and excitement. When the King returned from dinner, he retired immediately, as had been his wont for some time past, to his chamber. When alone and secure from intrusion, he and Charles set to work to complete the removal of the chief obstacle to their enterprise. With patient continued filing, the King had worked away entirely the iron at the top, concealing the gap with the lead that tied the glass, though at the bottom the filing still remained to be done, as any attempt there could not have been hidden, and must have led to discovery, but the iron had been constantly rubbed with aqua-fortis. It was now nine o'clock, and the King calculated by his former labours that it would take them an hour to sever it. The escape was fixed for eleven o'clock, and at a quarter to that hour the King was to emerge from his window in order to give him time to cross the bowling-green and make his way to the horses. Charles Harcourt took the instrument and worked steadily for half an hour. In the dead stillness of the night the noise of the file seemed to him fearfully distinct, and he trembled lest it should betray them. All of a sudden he felt the bar give in his hand, and had it not been secured by the lead at the top, it would have fallen forward into the chamber. The aqua-fortis had done its work in eating away the iron, and before it could have been expected their task was done. His Majesty was greatly pleased when he saw what had formerly been the fatal obstacle to his escape overcome. They now proceeded to tie the cords, by which the King was to descend, to the window-frame. Once or twice while thus employed Charles fancied he heard a rustling in the bushes below ; but the noise was so slight, it might only be a rabbit or a bird. The night also favoured their enterprise, for it was now perfectly dark. In the early part of their operations there had been a bright moon and Charles had now and then paused to view by its pale silver light the bowling-green below, on which the long dark shadows of the trees and part of the rugged outline of the massive keep were cast, to try if he could discover anything of the treacherous design which he feared was silently accompanying them step by step in their undertaking. No, he could discern nothing ; only the sentinels kept watch, walking up and down with even tramp. Then he heard the voices of those who came to relieve guard, and Charles knew that the King's friends were now on duty, and that in a few more minutes the time would be come. He went up to the King and said:

"Your Majesty will permit me to descend first from the window, to try the cords if they are sufficiently firm and strong ? "

"I do not like you to encounter that risk for me," said the King, in his kindest tones.

"Sire, I implore you, as a favour, to permit me to do this."

"Be it as you wish, then," said the King. "You have served me too well and too faithfully for me to refuse what you ask of ɪ e as a favour."

The grea ɪr risk, which was uppermost in Charles's mind, had ɪ ot even occurred to him, or he would never have consented to this request. He was only thinking of the security of the cords when he objected to Charles's proposal, which, on reflection, he thought would be less likely to break with the boy's slight form hanging on them than with his own heavier weight.

"Sire," said Charles once again, "will you give me your blessing ? "

He knelt down, and the King could scarcely command his voice as he said, laying his hand upon the head of his faithful servant—

"The Lord Himself be thy keeper, the Lord be thy

defence upon thy right hand. The Lord shall preserve thee from all evil, yea, it is even He that shall keep thy soul."

When the King ceased speaking Charles seized his hand and kissed it with passionate affection, then, without further delay, sprang to the window, grasped the cord, and began the descent. It has been already said that the window was about ten feet from the ground. Charles was now within three feet of the end of the cord, and was about to wave his handkerchief, the sign agreed upon that it was safe for the King to follow his example, when there was a sudden sharp report of a pistol, the cord was severed, and young Harcourt dropped to the ground mortally wounded. Major Rolph,—for, as the poor lad had imagined, no one else could have been guilty of such brutal cowardice,—rushed from the bushes, thinking to find King Charles dead at his feet ; and when, instead of that well-known face and form, he saw a young lad, in the flower of his youth and strength, stretched on the ground he swore a fearful oath and turned sullenly away. " They have been too many for us, after all," he muttered ; " but at least their plan shall not succeed." And shouting " Treason ! " in a moment all the soldiers were collected on the spot. The sentinels who were on duty knew what had occurred, and were filled with admiration for young Harcourt's brave conduct, and with grief for his sad fate. Dowcett at once ran up to him, and took his cold hand in his, and felt his heart.

" He is not dead yet," he said. " He must be taken directly to his mother. It is Charles Harcourt. Some one fetch the Governor ! "

" He is right away on the other side of the castle," sneered Rolph, " and he had his reasons for going there. I am commander-in-chief in his absence. Here some of you," he said, addressing the soldiers, " follow me to the

King's apartments, lest he should make his escape while we stand gaping here."

In vain had his Majesty strained his eyes to pierce the thick darkness. He had heard the shot, but he did not know that it had proved fatal to his faithful servant. He only knew that they were betrayed, and that all was at an end; but anxiety to know if Charles had been hurt overcame every feeling of disappointment on his own account, and when a troop of soldiers, headed by Major Rolph, burst without ceremony into his apartment, his first inquiry was for Charles. " Was he wounded ? "

" Serve the young traitor right," growled the villain ; but one of the soldiers, who had been a sentinel below the King's window that night, saluted him with profound respect and said, in a low voice, " Please your Majesty, he is not dead." The King gave him a look of gratitude which he never forgot, and that soldier did not see him again till the terrible 30th of January, when he made his way through vast crowds of people to ask God's blessing on that Royal head and gaze for the last time on that noble form.

The noise and confusion in the castle brought the Governor back from the battlements, where he had retired, hoping not to be summoned till he could be apprised that the task which had been such a heavy burden to him was at an end. Worked upon by Major Rolph's violent threats, a reluctant consent had been wrung from him ; but his conscience had been ill at ease, and had it not been for Rolph's persistent representations of the incalculable service which would be rendered to the kingdom at large, and that he had cause to know the King himself was weary of his life, he would not have yielded. When he perceived, on reaching the scene of action, what had really occurred, he nearly swooned on the spot.

" Alice ! " he exclaimed, in an agony of despair ;
" she will never forgive me, she will curse me ! " And
then he shouted to the soldiers, " Here, bring a stretcher !
blankets from my own room ! summon the garrison
surgeon, and let the youth be conveyed to Madam ——.
No, not there, to Dr. Russell's lodging. Lift him tenderly ; he is not dead," he said, anxiously, to the surgeon,
who was already there and had been administering a
cordial to the dying boy.

" He is not dead," said the surgeon, gravely ; " but
he has only a few hours to live."

Charles opened his eyes : " My mother," he murmured,
faintly, " take me to her."

Ever since his grandson's departure that afternoon,
Dr. Russell had been anxiously revolving in his mind the
probabilities of success which might attend that night's
enterprise. When he was roused from his study, where
he was writing at midnight, by a loud knock, and heard
the sound of men's voices outside, a horrible surmise of
what had happened crossed his mind before he opened
the door and saw his grandson's apparently lifeless
form stretched on a litter. The surgeon advanced
respectfully, seeing the horror and grief in the good
priest's face, which deprived him of all power of
speech.

" He is not dead, sir," he said, " but wounded, I fear,
mortally. He has asked for his mother, and he has not
many hours to live."

Dr. Russell asked no questions, he saw no time was to
be lost. " Follow me," he said to the men who were
bearing the litter ; then to himself he murmured, " God
help my poor Alice ! "

He touched Charles's hand, he breathed upon his lips,
and felt his heart : it beat faintly, but there was no
sign of consciousness ; the blue eyes never opened, till

K

his mother fell on her knees in a passion of grief beside the bed where they had laid him.

"Charles, my boy, my darling!" she cried; "speak to me, my brave, noble boy! you have saved the King; but O my darling, at the sacrifice of your own life."

"Is the King safe?" said Charles; he opened his eyes and saw his mother. "Mother, dearest mother, do not grieve for me; how could I do otherwise? they would have killed him, and now he is safe and——" he looked anxiously at his grandfather, "free!"

They scarcely dared to tell him that this was not so; but they could not deceive him.

"Not to-night, dear boy," said Dr. Russell, gently; "but soon, we trust. Let us leave it in the hands of God. If it had not been for your noble act, to-morrow's sun would have brought mourning to the whole kingdom."

Charles, who now felt his end coming very near, for the ball had lodged in his side, and he was bleeding fast internally, asked his grandfather to pray for him. Frances and his mother remained by him, controlling, for his sake, their emotion as best they could.

About four o'clock the day began to break, the sun rose, and through the open window came the song of the birds and the fragrant smell of the blossoms.

"Mother," said Charles, "stoop down quite close to me"; and then, in a low voice, often interrupted with painful gasps for breath, he told her of his doubts and fears, how God had strengthened him and how happy he felt now. "I should like to see Arthur and John once again," he added, after a short pause.

Just then footsteps were heard below, and Frances looked out of window. "There they are," she said, eagerly.

Yes, through Edward Worsley and Dowcett they had heard it all, and, regardless of their own risk, for Major

Rolph had sent out troops to capture all who had taken
any part in the escape,—they had come to see Charles
and to thank him for having saved the King. Charles
brightened at their glowing words of praise, and when
Arthur, who had not understood till then that the wound
was mortal, and that his brother was dying, burst into
an uncontrollable passion of sobs, Charles put his hand
upon his head, bowed low with grief.

"Arthur," he said, " my dear brother, you would not
grieve for me if you could guess at the thousandth part
of my happiness ; you would have done the same had
you been in my place. Be a good son to mother ; you
and John," and he smiled faintly, " will be her only sons
now. I need not say fight for the King, for I know you
to be a true son of our father, and that you will spend
your last drop of blood in his service. Tell him he was
in my thoughts to the last ; and when he is free and,
please God, restored to his throne, ask his Majesty not
to forget dear mother, for my sake."

Then a change came over him ; he raised himself
with a sudden effort to kiss Madam Harcourt, whispering
once again to her, " The Psalm, mother, we heard yesterday morning—ask grandfather to read it to me now."

Dr. Russell began, in his full rich voice : " The King
shall rejoice in Thy strength, O Lord, exceeding glad
shall he be of Thy salvation " ; but when he came to
the verse, " For Thou shalt give him everlasting felicity,
and make him glad with the joy of Thy countenance,"
a beautiful smile came over Charles's face, a slight con-
vulsive shudder ran through his frame, he grasped his
mother's hand, and fell back—dead.

It would be in vain to attempt to depict the grief and
anguish of mind which followed upon Charles Harcourt's
death. Madam Harcourt must have sunk under it, had
it not been for her own lively faith in her father's tender

care. By and by, as healing came with time, she was
able to take pride in his having died to save the King,
and to rejoice that he was taken away from the evil to
come, for, had he lived to see the 30th of January in the
following year, when the life of sorrows of his loved
master culminated in his martyrdom, his heart must
have broken, and, like many witnesses of that barbarous
murder, of whom it is recorded in history, he would have
dropped down dead on the spot.

There is some satisfaction in knowing that Major
Rolph, although he did not meet with the fate which he
deserved, suffered several months' rigorous imprisonment.

Colonel Hammond discovered, when too late, the fatal
mistake which he had made in allowing his self-interest
to overrule his sense of duty, and retired in shame and
disgrace from his post, not having sufficiently served the
interests of his employers, in spite of his disloyal conduct
towards his lawful sovereign.

And the King——

But there is no need to recall the melancholy details
of the few remaining months of life which were allowed
to him before that deed of violence and injustice was
wrought, which excited universal indignation at the
time, and which, although more than two centuries have
elapsed since it was perpetrated, can never be spoken of
without a thrill of horror and shame.

The solemn Service appointed to be read in memory
of the Martyr King has borne, till a very recent period,
yearly witness to the patience and manifold virtues which
he displayed amid his sufferings, while from one of its
most beautiful prayers we learn that " by that barbarous
murder (as on this day) committed upon the sacred person
of Thine anointed, neither the greatest of kings, nor the
best of men, are more secure from violence than from

natural death. Teach us also hereby," the prayer con-
tinues, " so to number our days that we may apply our
hearts unto wisdom. And grant that neither the splen-
dour of anything that is great, nor the conceit of anything
that is good in us, may withdraw our eyes from looking
upon ourselves as sinful dust and ashes, but that, according to the example of this Thy blessed martyr, we may
press forward to the prize of the high calling that is
before us, in faith and patience, humility and meekness,
mortification and self-denial, charity and constant
perseverance unto the end."

CHAPTER IX

" O the twenty-ninth of May,
It was a glorious day
When the King did enjoy his own again ! "

Cavalier Song.

THERE are certain events in history which leave an indelible impression upon our minds. They stand forth in definite shapes among the shadowy outlines of the past, and although the incidents of the actual moment may so fill our thoughts as to exclude, for the time, all other considerations, yet as the excitement which they bring with them subsides, these former events rise up again in all their vigour. Time cannot destroy them, for they appeal to that nobler and better part of our nature which, born to immortality, is able to resist temporal influence.

The Restoration may be looked upon as one of these landmarks in history, for it bears upon its face that stamp of poetical justice which is dear to every generous mind. That the English, as a nation, had no part in the murder of their King, but that, on the contrary, it filled them with grief and indignation, is clearly proved from history. Hume says : " Never monarch in the full triumph of success and victory was more dear to his people than his misfortunes and magnanimity, his patience and piety, had rendered this prince."* And Clarendon : " It is most certain that in that very hour when he was thus wickedly murthered in the sight of the

* Hume, Vol. VII, p. 148.

sun, he had as great a share in the hearts and affections of his subjects, was as much beloved, esteemed, and longed for by the people in general as any of his predecessors had been."*

The festivities and rejoicings at the Restoration find no parallel in England's annals either before or afterwards. " When Charles II landed, the cliffs of Dover were covered with thousands of gazers, among whom scarcely one could be found who was not weeping with delight. The journey to London was a continued triumph. The whole road from Rochester was bordered by booths and tenants, and looked like an interminable fair. Everywhere flags were flying, bells and music sounding, wine and ale flowing in rivers to the health of him whose return was the return of peace, of law, and of freedom."† And because this enthusiasm was as much produced by the conviction that a great wrong was thus being righted, so far as it was possible, as by the immediate benefits which were expected to accrue to the country with the Restoration, it has not passed away, but still, as the anniversary recurs, it never fails to bring with it a throb of pleasure to every loyal heart.

It will be necessary to cast one brief glance over the eleven years which elapsed before this happy consummation was effected, in order to follow the fortunes of the loyal family whose history is related in these pages.

Most of those who had taken part in the attempted escape of the 28th of May, in which poor Charles Harcourt lost his life, managed to avoid being captured by Colonel Hammond's soldiers ; but John Newland was apprehended and imprisoned for a short time. On regaining his liberty, he did not leave England so long as the smallest chance remained of assisting the unfortunate

* Clarendon's *Hist. of the Rebellion*, Vol. V, Book XI, p. 209.
† Macaulay's *Hist. of England*, Vol. I, p. 150.

King. When all was over, and the hopes of the Royalists
were dashed to the ground by his cruel murder, young
Newland fled to offer his services to the young King, who
was then at the Hague. Arthur Harcourt accompanied
him, being now old enough to fulfil his long-cherished
desire of fighting for the Royal cause.

Meanwhile Madam Harcourt, with her daughter and
Dr. Russell, had their full share of suffering in those evil
times. Colonel Hammond, who would gladly have done
anything to make up for the irreparable loss of which he
had been as much the cause, from his weakness and
selfishness, as Major Rolph from wanton brutality, was
powerless to assist them, so strict a watch was kept upon
him by the Parliament. In a short time, knowing that
he had for ever forfeited his last chance of regaining
Madam Harcourt's esteem, he ceased even to endeavour
to help them during the few months he was allowed to
retain the governorship of the island.

The times were indeed hard for all who remained faithful to the King. When he was at length forcibly carried
away from the castle, Dr. Russell, Madam Harcourt, and
her daughter, had to fly for their lives. The troops which
had been sent in numbers to accomplish this purpose
were quartered in the village, and showed themselves so
bitter towards the Royalists, especially to those who had
ministered to the King in his captivity, that it was no
longer safe for the Harcourts to remain in Carisbrook.
Dr. Russell only survived this treatment to die of a broken
heart when he heard of the fatal deed of the 30th of
January.

Madam Harcourt and Frances were thus left alone to
struggle as best they could against the perils and difficulties which surrounded them. Constant anxiety was
added to their troubles, for it was not easy in those days
to obtain tidings of the only two who remained to them

BURIAL OF KING CHARLES I THE MARTYR IN ST. GEORGE'S CHAPEL, WINDSOR.

AFTER C. W. COPE, R.A.

facing p. 152.

out of the little band of Carisbrook loyalists. They did
not leave the Isle of Wight, as they were destitute of
means wherewith to travel. For some little time they
were courteously entertained at Gatcombe by the father
of Edward Worsley; but when the news came of that
gallant young gentleman's death in battle at Worcester,
Gatcombe became a house of mourning. Soon afterwards
it was seized upon by the Parliament, but not before old
Mr. Worsley had been taken to his rest. Madam Harcourt and her daughter were thus once more homeless,
and in a state of horrible uncertainty as to whether
Arthur and John Newland had not shared the fate of
their brave companion.

But their anxiety on this point was relieved, after
some weeks of deep anguish of mind, by the return of
their faithful servant Nicholas, who, despite his age and
infirmities, had begged hard to accompany his young
master. Together they had fought desperately at
Worcester, where, before they would yield to superior
numbers, the Royalists were cut to pieces, and the streets
of the city were strewn with dead. Old Nicholas now
made his way back to the Isle of Wight, having seen the
King safely embarked at Shoreham, in Sussex, with his
young master and Mr. John Newland. This time he was
the bearer of good tidings to his mistress, and, as there
was no more fighting to be done for the King, he was
content to stay with her and share her poverty.

Madam Harcourt and Frances continued to pray for
those they loved, and to wait patiently for those better
days which came in God's own good time.

Again it was the month of May, sweet with the delicious
fragrance of the blossoms and joyous with the song of
the birds, like the memorable May of twelve years back,
which had never faded from their minds. Now it brought
joy instead of sorrow, for, on the 8th, King Charles the

Second was proclaimed with great solemnity in Palace Yard, at Whitehall, and at Temple Bar, and then a gallant fleet was sent to convey him from Holland; but before he disembarked at Dover, Madam Harcourt and Frances had each received a letter. Madam Harcourt's was to this effect:

"DEAREST MOTHER,

"All has come right at last. The King will enjoy his own again. But you must come to Dover to see him arrive, for they say there never was such a gallant sight as it will be. Come with Frances, that I may see your dear faces as the best part of all the welcome when we land. God be thanked for all His mercies!

"Your affectionate son, half crazed with joy,

"ARTHUR HARCOURT."

And Frances' letter—we need not ask from whom it came, or what were its contents, but certainly her invitation to Dover was not less pressing than the one her mother had received. No time was to be lost; their preparations were soon made, and we need scarcely add that they were among those who "wept with delight," as Lord Macaulay tells us, when the King landed on his native shores.

The joy of the meeting of mother and son, of Frances and her lover, after those long years of separation, will be more easily imagined than described.

Sorrow and anxiety had left their traces upon Madam Harcourt's patient face, and had silvered her hair, but there was the same sweet smile, the same gentle, loving eyes, and Arthur, as he kissed her again and again, vowed that she was not the least altered, and that no beauty could vie with her.

Frances, at twenty-seven, was as lovely and winning

as she had been at sixteen. Perhaps there was an expression of greater firmness about her mouth than when she had trembled at Colonel Hammond's unexpected question, but her eyes had the same look of modest trustfulness which had first captivated John Newland. To him she seemed, if possible, more perfect than ever. Her image had always been present to him throughout all the battles and hardships which he had undergone. To serve the King, and make himself more worthy of her, had been the two dearest objects of his ambition, and now that he felt he had fairly won her, he took her hand, and rapturously gazed upon her beautiful face.

" You were right, dearest," he said, " to bid me wait. I was not worthy of you then,—indeed, I never shall be, though I've tried very hard."

" It was not that, John," said Frances, gently ; " you were always much too good for me. I have suffered greatly, but I knew it was best to wait ; and now in the joy of this moment all the sad past seems to have vanished away."

" My darling ! " said John.

Then there was the meeting between brother and sister ; and John seized the opportunity to say beseechingly to Madam Harcourt : " You will let me be your son now ? "

The next day Arthur and John accompanied the King on his road to London, and Madam Harcourt and Frances followed them.

On the 29th of May, which was the King's birthday, his Majesty entered London. The streets were thronged with people, flags waved from every house, every balcony was filled with eager faces, enthusiastic cheers rent the air, while the bells rang in clamorous peals.

" The concourse was so great, that the King rode in a crowd from the bridge to Whitehall, all the Companies of the City standing in order on both sides, and giving loud thanks to God for his Majesty's presence. He no sooner came to Whitehall, but the two Houses of Parliament solemnly cast themselves at his feet, with all vows of affection and fidelity to the world's end."*

Madam Harcourt and Frances were among the joyful witnesses of this triumphal entry; but while the King was receiving the addresses of the Houses of Parliament, they turned their steps towards Westminster Abbey, where a special service of thanksgiving was being offered up for the happy restitution of the King and Royal family.

Once again, after many years' disuse, the rites proceed: the sacred sounds rise and fall in rich cadence throughout that glorious pile, where so many of England's Kings sleep their last sleep. Although their bodies are dust beneath their mouldering tombs, may not their souls have rejoiced that one of their noble line was thus triumphantly restored to the throne of his fathers?

Again the organ peals forth in one joyous burst of praise, while clear and distinct the words of the Psalm rise above: "The king shall rejoice in Thy strength, O Lord, exceeding glad shall he be of Thy salvation."

In an instant Madam Harcourt was carried back to the little room at Carisbrook, to her darling boy as he lay dying on his bed, his blue eyes fastened on her, as her father read those glorious words of hope and trust; and she sank down, entirely overcome by the recollection.

"Mother, dearest mother," whispered Frances, "it is all as he would have wished now. The King's own son is on the throne of his father, while the King for whom Charles died has the martyr's crown of pure gold upon his head, and——"

She paused; for again the full-voiced choir took up

* Clarendon's *History of the Rebellion*, Vol. VI, p. 772.

the triumphant strain : " He asked life of Thee and Thou gavest him a long life, even for ever and ever."

But little more remains to be told. We have it upon historical record that Charles the Second, worthless and ungrateful as he was, made a point of faithfully rewarding all those persons who had ministered to his father during his captivity at Carisbrook. In the case of the Harcourts, there was an additional reason for this, on account of the gallant services for which he was personally indebted to them.

Arthur remained in his Majesty's Body Guard, where he was promoted to be a colonel ; but John Newland left the army and retired to his place in the Isle of Wight, —the place which had once belonged to Madam Harcourt, and which his father had purchased from her when she was in such distress. As soon as it became his, John at once offered to restore it to her, but Madam Harcourt declined the offer ; and as it had been long ago agreed that, whenever Frances married, her mother was to share her home, everything was thus happily arranged.

Before they left London, John and Frances were married. Weddings have been so often described at the conclusion of every tale that has ever been written, that it would be a tedious repetition to dwell upon this one. It shall only be mentioned that Frances, true to her principles, wore a chaplet of oak-leaves mingled with white roses,—the badge of that party whose cause she, with all those who were dear to her, had laboured so perseveringly to support.

After the wedding they all went back together to the home where, before evil times came upon them, they had lived so happily. It was only a mile from Carisbrook, and Madam Harcourt's first care was to visit her son's grave in the churchyard. Hitherto his place of rest had only been marked by a mound of green turf ; any attempt at ornament would have been speedily defaced by the fanatical hands of the Puritans. But now Madam Harcourt caused a richly-carved oak cross to be placed over the grave, and at the foot of the cross was the following inscription :

" ' Fear God, Honour the King ! '

IN MEMORY OF

CHARLES HARCOURT,

Aged 18,

Who was killed May 29, 1648, in attempting to forward the escape of His Sacred Majesty, Charles I, from Carisbrook Castle.

' Be thou faithful unto death, and I will give thee a crown of life.' "

THE END

The Mayflower Press, Plymouth. William Brendon & Son, Ltd.

www.ingramcontent.com/pod-product-compliance
Lightning Source LLC
Chambersburg PA
CBHW031127210626
46816CB00015B/1120